OUTSTANDING 1

"a major pioneer of street fiction" (*Library Journal*)

AND HER NOVELS

DUTCH

"Almost unparalleled in its shock value...thoroughly absorbing...a fast-moving story with ruthless dialogue...vividly highlights the crime-riddled existence of notorious Newark gangster Bernard James, aka Dutch...will keep any lover of this genre captivated."   —The RAWSISTAZ Reviewers

"A bone-chilling story of murder, violence, and the struggle for power. It is a harrowing tale."   —MyShelf.com

ALIBI

"The classic investigative query—'Where were you on the night in question?'—allows Woods to once again prove why she's in a league of her own."   —*Philadelphia Tribune*

"Gritty...While giving a sympathetic voice to her financially desperate heroine...Woods observes that easy cash comes with a steep price."   —*Library Journal* (starred review)

"Woods writes with feeling and a strong sense of Philadelphia setting...Fast-paced and exciting, *Alibi* is an action-filled story about the desperate life of one urban girl and the consequences of trying to break away."   —*Booklist*

"Blistering...This wickedly satisfying page-turner will leave readers eager for the next installment." —*Publishers Weekly*

"Woods has established herself as the Queen of Urban Fiction...launching a revolution in reading...Her hustle made real the dream of every wannabe author, the fantasy that your work will inspire a generation, will create a wave of response and thought, that posits you as a leader and a vanguard of a movement all your own." —Heavy.com

"A fast-paced, action-filled page-turner." —MyShelf.com

"Gritty drama that only Woods can deliver...[she] writes with the suspense and ingenuity of a crime novelist and has crafted a literary adrenaline rush for mystery, thriller, and urban fiction fans alike." —The RAWSISTAZ Reviewers

"An engaging thriller with an intricate plot."
—BlackVoices.com

"A fast-paced read...Teri Woods is quite a good writer."
—*Sacramento Book Review*

TRUE TO THE GAME III
"Vividly depicts the 1990s drug culture...urban fiction fans will welcome the melodramatic final entry in bestseller Woods's True to the Game trilogy." —*Publishers Weekly*

TRUE TO THE GAME II
"Raw...gutsy." —*Essence*

"Explosive...excellent...masterful...A must-have...definitely worth waiting for...solidifies Ms. Woods's place as one of the Queens of Street Lit."   —The RAWSISTAZ Reviewers

"Four out of five...Wonderful...a great story...a fast-paced, exciting read that will surely keep you on your toes."

—Urban-Reviews.com

DUTCH III
International Gangster

TERI WOODS

GRAND CENTRAL
PUBLISHING

NEW YORK   BOSTON

Grand Central Publishing
Hachette Book Group
237 Park Avenue
New York, NY 10017

www.HachetteBookGroup.com

Printed in the United States of America

First Edition: May 2011

10 9 8 7 6 5 4 3 2 1

Grand Central Publishing is a division of Hachette Book Group, Inc.
The Grand Central Publishing name and logo is a trademark of Hachette Book Group, Inc.

Library of Congress Cataloging-in-Publication Data

Woods, Teri.
    Dutch III : international gangster / Teri Woods.—1st ed.
      p. cm.
    ISBN 978-0-446-55154-0
    1. African Americans—Fiction. 2. Gangsters—Fiction. I. Title. II. Title: Dutch 3. III. Title: Dutch three.
    PS3573.O6427D88 2011
    813'.54—dc22
                                                                    2010032859

PROLOGUE
Begin Again

One Month Ago

Craze sat in the parking lot of the Essex County Courthouse. He sparked a blunt and cracked his window. *There's so much riding on this,* he thought to himself anxiously. He had been nervous ever since Dutch's trial began. All his planning and all his preparation was about to pay off. Either Dutch would escape or he was already a dead man trying. Either way, there was no turning back.

Craze puffed the blunt, thinking of Qwan and his testimony. He hadn't seen him in years. *A preacher. Ain't that nothing? This nigga went from gangster to God.* It had only been a minute, but time erased no pages from Craze's book. With Dutch on trial for what the media had dubbed "the Month of Murder," and Roc and Angel locked up, Craze was now the commander in charge. He had become the ears and eyes that Dutch didn't have, being locked up and behind bars. *No one has a clue how this shit is about to go down.* He had spent the past month devising the most brilliant of getaway capers. *It'll go down in the history books as one of the all-time greatest escapes ever.* The question of how to save Dutch from going to prison for the rest of his life had consumed him. One thing was for sure, Craze would rather bust Dutch out of a courthouse than bust him out of a maximum-security prison, and that was exactly what he planned to do.

Behind the rap music of Nas, Foxy, and AZ playing in the background, Craze heard his phone ringing. He picked it up to see who was calling, but the phone's tiny monitor read "private number." He decided to pass, but before he could set the phone down, it rang again. And again he ignored the call. But the private number wouldn't go away. His phone rang a fifth and sixth time. *What if it's Dutch calling?* That wasn't how they communicated, and Craze knew that. Dutch never liked phones.

"Them phones are trouble. Whatever you do, don't call me, understand?"

If Dutch hadn't said it once, he had said it a thousand times. The phone had rung for the ninth time when Craze decided to see who was calling.

"Yeah," he answered, calm and cool, as if the phone hadn't been ringing nonstop for the last five minutes straight.

"Mr. Shaw, I presume?" The voice was new to him, distant but familiar, carrying a thick French accent.

"That depends on who wants to know," Craze answered, looking around the parking lot for anything or anyone who seemed suspicious.

"Yes...I see...Mr. Shaw it is. I have a proposition for you."

"Well, ah, before you start proposing, you think you might want to identify yourself?"

"If you want to keep Dutch from spending the rest of his

life behind bars, meet me at the St. Regis Hotel in New York City. Come to the penthouse suite, midnight tonight, and Mr. Craze...come alone."

"Who's this?" Craze quickly questioned before the line went dead.

He put the phone down and looked around the parking lot. It was quiet and still. He started the engine to the Porsche and put the car in drive.

If you want to keep Dutch from spending the rest of his life behind bars, meet me at the St. Regis Hotel in New York City, the voice rang over and over in his head, the accent escaping him each time. The call traveled with him as his Porsche glided down the streets of Newark. He looked at the time. It was ten-forty-five. If he was going to take the caller's meeting at midnight, he didn't have much time.

He picked up his phone.

"Meet me on the corner of Clinton Avenue and Bergen. I need backup," Craze ordered before hanging up the phone.

With several Charlies in place, he entered the St. Regis Hotel on Fifty-fifth Street, off Fifth Avenue. He walked past a Charlie in the lobby as if she was a stranger, went straight to the elevators, and pressed P for the penthouse suite. He had two Charlies accompanying him, side by side, guns loaded. Craze got off the elevator leery and looking for any signs of trouble. He walked down the hallway to two double cherry-stained oak doors marked "Penthouse" in gold lettering. He knocked at the door.

"Let's get this party started," he said to the Charlies as he breathed a deep sigh at the unknown behind the double doors.

A few moments later, a short, dark-skinned man opened the door.

"Come in," he said, allowing them all to enter the room. Standing vigil across the floor were eight straight-backed members of a security detail in black suits. They looked as if killing was just as natural to them as brushing their teeth.

"Mr. Shaw, I see you aren't too good on following directions," said a tall, thin African man wearing a dashiki. "I do believe I asked you to come alone." The man extended his hand to Craze, who looked at it, then calmly took the man's hand in his.

"I'm still waiting on the introduction," said Craze, bending his head slightly and looking the African point-blank in the eye.

"My name is Joseph Odouwo," he said, smiling as he watched Craze's reaction turn to complete uncertainty. The Charlies standing next to him became nervous as well. Craze knew exactly who he was now in the presence of. Joseph Odouwo was Kazami's uncle, his very rich and very powerful uncle. Craze quickly reached for his gun and pointed it at Odouwo's head as Odouwo's henchmen pulled their weapons out and pointed them at Craze and the Charlies. The Charlies standing on either side of Craze also had their weapons drawn and were pointing them in the direction of Odouwo's henchmen, who were spread about the room.

"Oh, dear, I was afraid this would happen," said Odouwo, shaking his head.

"*Mettez vos pistolets vers le bas. Mettez-les loin,*" he ordered his men in their native tongue.

"See, Mr. Shaw," said Odouwo, lifting his hands and waving to his men around the room. He wanted Craze to feel comfortable, wanted to offer a sign of peace. He carefully watched the floor as his men withdrew their weapons.

"What did you ask me to come here for, Mr. Odouwo?" Craze said, lowering his weapon and looking around the room, making sure there were no more guns pointed at his head.

"*Svp, laissez-nous,* leave us," said Odouwo to his loyal and trusting henchman Zemi. The other members of his security team began exiting the room. Craze watched them leave one by one.

"May we speak alone, Mr. Shaw? I promise you, I mean you no harm here," Odouwo said as he took a few steps back before seating himself on the sofa.

Craze looked at the two Charlies and nodded. "It's okay."

"We'll be right outside the door," the Charlies agreed as they left the room.

"Okay, so you got me to yourself. What's this all about?" asked Craze, wanting to get to the bottom line.

"Please, have a seat. May I get you a refreshing beverage? Coke, Sprite—or would you care for a spirit?" Odouwo asked politely, smiling and intertwining his fingers as he spoke.

Craze was becoming impatient. Odouwo sensed it and poured the can of Coke he was holding in his hand into a small glass of ice before taking a sip.

"I am Kazami's uncle," he stated matter-of-factly. "If I'm not mistaken, it was Dutch and you and his other faithful and loyal cohorts who killed my nephew. Am I correct?" Mr. Odouwo politely asked.

"Mr. Odouwo...you must understand..."

Before he could say another word, Odouwo cut him off. "I understand completely. No one could get at this man!" he said with excitement, now standing above Craze. "How you did it is beyond me. I want you to know that at first, I was upset, but after the death of Kazami our family learned of certain matters..."

Joseph Odouwo thought carefully as he spoke and calmed himself as he sat back down next to Craze. The personal business of his family was best left personal. "Let's just say Kazami was planning the assassination of his father, my brother, and had that happened, I would be left powerless. I would have nothing. It was his plan. Dutch and his cohorts became my biggest allies when they killed him. Little did I know, but because of you, I am in the position that I am in, and my family is very grateful, very grateful indeed," he said, holding up his glass as if cheering Craze for a job well done.

"So, you owe me, Odouwo. It sounds like I helped save your life."

"Yes, my friend, very much so," he joked. "I must say, though," he quickly added, "Mr. James is a man that will go to any lengths to get what he wants or, in this case, to get who he wanted. By far, my nephew was no easy target. You could ask the Italian mob that. They failed many times. But that Dutch... he was successful," Odouwo said with a baleful grin on his face before taking another sip at his drink.

"Mr. Odouwo, I'm glad that we were of great assistance to you and your family. However, my man is facing life in prison," said Craze, really wanting to get down to the gist of why Odouwo had summoned him.

"I know this, and I also know that over the years, Dutch has inherited many enemies. Once he goes to jail, it is a guarantee that he will be dead within twenty-four hours. The Italian Mafia will see to that. I'm the only person that can help Mr. James. I want to offer him a chance at life. All I ask is for a favor in return," said Odouwo.

Craze sat back, curious as to how Odouwo could help Dutch, when it was he who had already devised the perfect plan.

"Who says we need your help?" Craze asked.

"Even if he escapes from prison, which is highly possible, what would he do? Where would he go?" asked Odouwo.

That was the one thing Craze hadn't figured out yet. But he was working on it.

"Mr. Shaw, I can see that you doubt my influence, but I assure you my affiliations are with the most powerful political figures in the world. I have connections in every corner of the globe, and if I don't, trust me when I say, someone next to me does. I can get Mr. James out of the country, so he could start over. Do you know anyone else who can do that?" Odouwo asked with a hint of sarcasm, raising his brow.

Craze already knew that Dutch would never be able to live in the States once they busted him out. He would become America's Most Wanted. Getting Dutch out of the country had been the only obstacle in Craze's plan. Everything else was concrete. Craze had everything mapped out, even the getaway car they would use. But he didn't know where to take Dutch or what to do with Dutch once he freed him. They would be in a chase, a manhunt of sorts, and there could be no mishaps and no mixups. It sounded good, real good, what Odouwo was saying, but the question was, at what cost?

"You got my attention. What do you want Dutch to do?"

"I need Mr. James to do something very simple for me. I need someone killed," Odouwo said, as if it were as simple as picking up a loaf of bread from the grocery store.

"I think you already know that's what we do," said Craze, waiting for the punch line.

"Yes, so true." Odouwo smiled, loving the sense of confidence, the swagger, and the unrehearsed conversation. "Have you ever heard of Taji Tita?" asked Odouwo in his broad accent.

"No, who is he?"

"He is the president of my country, Nigeria."

Craze was baffled, *I know he don't think we killing the president of Nigeria. Is he crazy?* "Let me get this straight. You want Dutch to assassinate the president of Nigeria? Yo, you are bugging," joked Craze, now laughing at Odouwo as if the man was out of his mind. "Ain't nobody trying to kill no presidents. Man, oh, man!" said Craze, realizing what he had gotten himself into. He looked at Odouwo. The man's face was as straight as a wooden board.

"This is a very grave matter and it can and it must be done," said Odouwo in all seriousness.

"Why? Why must it be done?"

Joseph Odouwo stood up and walked over to the minibar. He poured himself another glass of soda and turned and faced Craze. "The president won't grant any of our citizens authorization to lease diamond fields in Sierra Leone. This has caused quite a bit of turmoil within our government. My uncle Yusef Odouwo is highly favored to be Nigeria's next president—that is, if something were to happen to Tita," Odouwo affirmed.

"So why Dutch? Out of all the people in the world, why him?" Craze questioned.

"Like I stated earlier, I am very impressed by how close Mr. James was able to get to Kazami. How ruthless he was in his attempt to gain power. I can appreciate him. But make no mistake, there are others that will do what needs to be done, especially for what I'm offering."

"And just exactly what are you offering?" asked Craze.

Odouwo reached into the inner pocket of his suit jacket and pulled out a small black velvet satchel. Carefully, he opened the pouch's drawstring tie and shook the contents into his hand. He showed Craze the biggest and brightest diamonds Craze had ever seen. Odouwo took Craze's hand and placed the diamonds in his palm. They sparkled and danced in the light. The diamonds gleamed "Say yes" at him, and he was in a daze as he turned them in his palm.

"What I am offering is not only the chance to save Mr. James's life, but a stake in my diamond trade. The stones in your hand cost merely pennies, but are worth millions of dollars. I play no games here today, Mr. Shaw. What I offer is a once-in-a-lifetime chance. If I were you, I would choose carefully." Odouwo beckoned as Craze sat quietly, still staring at the diamonds he held in the palm of his hand. Odouwo began to speak again. "You will leave the streets of Newark behind you?" Odouwo asked.

Craze thought of Roc and Angel; leaving them behind to rot in prison just didn't feel right.

"We got our people fighting to get out of—"

"That can be arranged," Odouwo interrupted, already knowing who he was speaking of. "It will take some time, but it can be done."

Craze looked at Odouwo and realized he was the real deal.

"So, Mr. Shaw, do we have a deal?" asked Odouwo, extending his hand across the table, hoping that Craze would do the right thing and accept the conditions of his offer.

Craze looked at the diamonds he was still holding in his hand, and what they had done all their lives in the streets of Newark just didn't equal that. He saw the potential to make more money than they had ever seen.

"You said a stake in your diamond trade?"

"A fifty-fifty stake in my diamond trade," Odouwo announced.

He looked back down at the palm of his hand and he thought of Dutch. *Dutch wouldn't refuse.* Craze shook Odouwo's hand and the deal was sealed.

"Now, let us get down to business and figure out a master plan." Odouwo smiled.

ROCK 'N ROLL BABY

Before leaving the hotel, Mr. Odouwo gave Craze one of the diamonds, encouraging Craze to think that not only could he be trusted, but he was putting an offer on the table that was more than worth its weight in gold. Craze, of course, wanted to see what it was really worth, so the very next morning, he tunneled through the Lincoln and took the stone to Jacob the Jeweler. The stone was appraised and was valued at over a million dollars.

"Nice." The infamous jeweler smiled as he placed the precious stone in a petite red velvet pouch and handed it back to Craze. "Very nice indeed."

It was then that Craze was convinced that Odouwo could be trusted. *Who would just hand me this diamond if it wasn't worth all this?* It was then that he also began to believe that Odouwo was a man of his word. Together they would formulate a plan to make sure that Dutch escaped, a free man. Craze had already masterminded the perfect plot. Besides, how hard could taking over a courthouse actually be?

Alex Kelly was a maintenance and janitorial aide at the Essex County Courthouse. Alex was a middle height Irishman with orangish-red hair. He was knocking back shots at his favorite Irish pub, Skipper's, as he did every night after work, when Craze took a seat at the bar beside him.

The bartender, Joe, walked over to Craze as he sat down.

"What can I get for ya?" the husky Irishman asked.

"Give me a double shot of Belvedere, no ice."

While the bartender made his drink, Craze glanced over at Alex, who was heavily into what was on the tube, trying to figure out how to make small talk. He looked at the hard-working laborer, his eyes traveling up and down. *He looks like he needs a few more drinks.* Craze grinned, knowing he was about to present Alex with an offer he couldn't refuse. Just looking at the man's calloused hands, his tattered and worn shoes, and the holes in the knees of his pants, he knew Alex would jump at his offer. After the bartender came back with his drink, Craze turned to Alex.

"Damn, partna. I don't know how you can drink that brown stuff. More power to you though," Craze said, trying to break the ice, then tossed back his double.

"Believe it or not, I've been drinkin' this brown shit since I was fourteen. It ain't never been much to me," Alex explained.

"Naw, man, I can't do it. I drank that shit one time and was sick as hell. Somebody would have to pay me a million dollars to touch that lethal shit again."

"Damn, I would hate to see what you would do for ten," Alex said, smiling while shaking his head.

"So, tell me, my man. What would you be willing to do for a cool million?" Craze queried.

"Shiittt... for a million dollars I'd do damn near anything," Alex said, laughing while raising his glass. "That's why I play the lottery every day," he said, patting his pocket where his lottery tickets were safe and sound.

"Oh, do you now, Alex?" asked Craze, throwing the man's name out there to see if he was paying attention.

"Wait a minute. How the hell you know my name?" Alex asked, almost choking.

"That's really not important," said Craze, lifting his glass and taking the shot to the head, staring into the eyes of Alex Kelly as he whispered in his most secretive voice, "what matters is that you work at the Essex County Courthouse."

Alex had never seen Craze before in his life. He didn't know his face and he was unaware what his intentions were, but he didn't think it would hurt to find out.

"I'm sorry, my friend, but I didn't get your name," Alex said.

"Chris, but you can call me Craze. That's what everyone calls me."

"Okay, Craze. I've been at that damn place for over sixteen years and I still can't get a promotion. Who would be happy with that?" Alex asked.

"Well, I got a proposal for you, and if you can deliver, I promise you, you'll never have to work another day in your life."

Alex looked at him as if he was crazy.

"Never work another day in my life, yeah right."

"If I had a million dollars, I wouldn't work," replied Craze, throwing a million on the table with the roll of his tongue.

"Yeah, right, I know you must be pulling my leg. How many of those you done had?" asked Alex, referring to Craze's Belvedere.

Craze ignored the comment, focusing on what he was there for. "Naw, I'm not pulling nothing, least of all your leg. I have a job for you, an important job, to me. You're about the only person who can pull it off, too."

Alex looked confused, unsure of what he could possibly do for the man in front of him that could be of such value. But if this guy was serious, then so was he.

"Tell me whatcha talking about."

"All I need is a few things placed around the courthouse. That's it, simple."

Alex was uncomfortable about the proposition and signaled for the bartender. "Can I get another one?" Alex asked nervously, requesting another shot. He was reluctant, and he began to wonder what all this was about.

"Shit...a million dollars...I don't think I want to know what you want me to put in that courthouse for you."

"Naw, you probably don't," answered Craze as he sensed the man's reluctance and threw back another shot of Belvedere.

"Shucks, you really got me sitting on the edge of my seat over here. Tell me, are you talking explosives?" he asked, figuring that for a million dollars, he must want him to blow the place up or something.

"No, there's no explosives, relax. You don't have to worry about that. All you have to worry about is a million dollars and what you're going to do with it," responded Craze, knowing how to get the man's mind focused on what it needed to be focused on, which was collecting a million dollars for a job well done.

Alex thought quickly about the million dollars Craze kept rolling off the tip of his tongue, speaking as if it were nothing more than pocket change.

"That's a lot of money," thought Alex out loud, staring off into space and thinking about all the wonderful things he could do with his life if he had a million dollars.

"Not really, Alex, but it's enough for you to change your life," said Craze as he gave Alex something to influence his decision. "Here's a lil' something for your time this evening, partner," Craze said, handing him a manila envelope.

"My number's inside. You got until the end of the week to call me, you understand? Friday, all right, Alex?" Craze asked, throwing a fifty-dollar bill on the bar to settle his tab.

Alex took the folded manila envelope Craze passed to him. He peeked inside the envelope, which contained fifty one-hundred-dollar bills. Then he looked at Craze.

"Friday," said Craze as Alex looked into the envelope once more, unable to believe he had finally hit the jackpot in life.

"Jesus almighty, you're giving this to me," he said, quite astonished with the envelope and its contents. He looked at Craze, realizing he was dead ass; serious, that is.

Craze nodded at the man, then he left the pub. Alex took the money out of the envelope, unable to believe it. It was as if he had hit the lottery, and he had been trying to win all his life. *Five thousand dollars*, thought Alex as he held the bills in his hands, unable to believe his luck. He read Craze's name and looked at his phone number written on a piece of paper that was wrapped around the small stack of hundred-dollar bills.

I got the luck of a leprechaun in me, he thought, smiling to himself. *I really need this money right here*, he said, thinking about a pile of bills he had on his kitchen counter.

He had never had that much money at one time unless it was tax refund time, and even then he didn't get five thousand back. He felt like his life was changing for the better already. It would take him a hundred and one days of hard labor to make that much money at his job, based on his low hourly pay scale. He couldn't believe his luck. He thought about the million dollars he was offered for providing some simple "placement" assistance. *How hard could it be to put some things in the courthouse? For a million dollars, I don't think it would be that hard at all, nope, not hard at all. It sounds a little too good to be true. I wonder what he wants me to put inside the courthouse for him? It must be something really important to him, if he's willing to pay a million dollars.* He was the senior janitor, been working there the last sixteen years of his life, even though he had nothing to show for it. And while he had no idea what was really going on, he did have an idea of what one million dollars was.

Alex decided he wouldn't be passing up on the offer. How could he pass on that? Only a fool would, and Alex Kelly was nobody's fool. Not only that, he was ready to be a millionaire. He had dreamed of being rich and driving a fancy sports car and living in a big, beautiful home. He had worked all his life and he was tired of having nothing to show for it. If this stranger was serious, then so was he. He ordered another drink, threw it back, and placed his tab money on the bar before walking out the door five thousand dollars richer.

FRANKIE B FRANK

Two weeks before the trial of the century had begun, Frank Sorbonno, or Frankie Bonno as he was also known, was scheduled to meet with Joseph Odouwo. Frank had accepted the appointment assuming that they were going to end the bad blood between them. Now that Dutch was to be put out to pasture, the doors were opening for Frankie, and he had every intention of stepping through them.

Frank and his bodyguards walked into Odouwo's suite at the St. Regis, the same suite Craze had been invited to just weeks before. Frank walked into the massive suite and over to a table where Odouwo was sitting. Odouwo stood and the men shook hands. Odouwo extended his arm and pointed at a chair for Frank to take a seat. Frank sat down as Odouwo finished pouring them some wine, then he sat as well.

"I thank you, Mr. Sorbonno, for meeting with me, despite our past differences. I hope the fruits of this council will assuage any ill feelings between us," he said, raising his glass for a toast before sipping. "For years, we have had Mr. James's name written on our hearts...the part reserved for vengeance. Ojiugo Kazami was my nephew. He served our family well, and to know he died in such a way, because of a man such as Mr. James, well...is a blow to our pride, to say the very least. And we would have implemented swift justice had it not been for your people's protection. Yet, we knew it would only be a matter of time before someone more sympathetic to our concerns would take over, for a house divided cannot stand," said Mr. Odouwo, knowing the part Frank had played in Tony Cerone's death, but not revealing it.

Frankie raised his glass of wine again in testament to that which Odouwo preached.

"But it seems God has smiled on us, as I understand Mr. Cerone is no longer with us."

"Yeah, the bastard finally caught it." Frankie smiled, glad that the bastard had gotten what he deserved.

"So, what do you intend to do?" Mr. Odouwo asked, wondering if he was right about Frank's intentions.

"I wanna kill the little black son of a bitch!" Frank blurted out before realizing who he was talking to.

"No offense," Frank said, trying to clean it up.

"None taken." The Nigerian smiled, thinking that he should slit Frank's throat right at the table. He decided against it, then continued, "But, let me be honest, heroin is our biggest export—that is, after oil. We use the proceeds to fund our freedom fighters back in my country. So the trade here in New Jersey is important to us. Therefore, I ask that you leave the streets and Mr. James to us. While your vendetta is personal, ours is, shall I say, spiritual. In return, I invite you to Nigeria. It is a beautiful country, the most beautiful in the world. I invite you to partake of its splendor. There are many opportunities for a man such as yourself in my country." Mr. Odouwo smiled, knowing Frank had no choice but to agree with what he was saying.

Mr. Odouwo had Frank right where he wanted him. If Frank didn't agree he wouldn't make it to the lobby. Mr. Odouwo was well aware that it was Frankie Bonno who had had the two hits put out on his nephew, Ojiugo. Mr. Odouwo was going to ignore what had happened in the past as long as Frank didn't affect his future. He needed Bernard James to be left alone so he could get him to Nigeria for the assassination. Mr. Odouwo had no real commitment to ending his feud with the Italians. This meeting was just to set up a stall tactic. Mr. Odouwo had more to his plan than anyone would ever know.

Frank was pleased that he wouldn't have to go head to head with the Nigerians anymore. It had been Dutch who had caused an unlikely alliance to be struck based on their hatred of him. Frank stuck out his hand and the bargain was sealed. Frank would send Dutch to prison, while the Nigerians would send him to his grave, or so Frankie Bonno thought.

STRICTLY BUSINESS

The night before Dutch was to be sentenced, according to plan and as he had been instructed, Alex finished up his work as he normally did around eleven-thirty. The last worker to leave the courthouse before him was usually out by eleven o'clock. He checked the hallways of the courthouse, making sure everyone was gone for the night and the coast was clear. Earlier, he had placed a heavy-duty trash can by one of the exit doors. He left the door slightly ajar as he stepped outside, rolled the trash can inside, and then made sure the door was closed behind him. Inside the trash can was a duffel bag under two black trash bags filled with garbage. He took the duffel bag that Craze had given him, threw it over his back, and headed toward the ladies' bathroom. He went into one of the stalls and lifted the cover of the toilet, then drained all the water out of it.

He then reached into the duffel bag and pulled out three Uzi automatic weapons wrapped in plastic wrap and put them in the basin before replacing the lid on top. He then put tape over the toilet seat and placed an "Out of Order" sign on the outside of the stall, then repeated the same act in the next stall over, leaving only two stalls available for use.

He left the ladies' room, then went on to the courtroom where Dutch's trial had been taking place. He rolled his cart in and went up to the defense table. He made sure his plastic gloves were on tightly and pulled the last two guns out of the duffel bag. He taped the .40 caliber pistols under the table and left the courtroom.

Alex had done everything he had been instructed to do before leaving for the night. All he could think about was tomorrow and how he would be a million dollars richer. He knew that something big was going down, he just didn't know what. The trial was all over the news, in every newspaper, and the talk of the town. He figured Dutch and his cohorts were gonna try to make a run for it. He didn't have a clue that Dutch was planning to commit a massacre.

Lying on the top bunk in his cell, Dutch's mind wandered into tomorrow. His trial was now over and he, just like everyone, was expecting a guilty verdict. He was hoping and praying that everything was in place. No stone could be left unturned if they planned to escape victorious. *Please don't let Craze fuck this up. This nigga be smoking and shit; what if he forgets something? Everything could go wrong.* That's why Dutch never did drugs or consumed any type of alcoholic beverage. They impaired the bodily functions, or so he believed. *We can't afford to lose nobody or leave no one behind.* He started thinking of everything that could happen and everything that could go wrong. He figured that even if everything fell through, certainly tonight would be his last night in jail. One way or another he knew he wasn't coming back to this cell. Dutch smiled and went to sleep.

TAKE THAT, HOLD THAT

It was early morning when the jury finally reached its verdict. Dutch had stood trial for what the media had dubbed the "trial of the century," and now it was time to face a jury of peers and find out if they would deem him guilty or innocent.

The courtroom was packed with everyone from the young to the old. Most of the spectators were there to see the look on Dutch's face when the jury came back and found him guilty. They wanted to see Dutch fry in hell. Very few were there to see him be acquitted of all charges and set free—no, that could simply be a nightmare. The streets would have no rest if that man walked out of the courtroom a free man. Newark had taken a toll from the Month of Murder. People were still scared to go outside. Looking around the courtroom at all the faces, no one would have ever thought that the little old ladies dressed up like grandmas going to an apple-pie-baking convention were about to bring the rain, but they were and no one in the courtroom was ready for what was about to happen. The Charlies had already been to the bathroom for their guns, and now it was just a matter of time before things popped off. Craze was parked outside the courthouse waiting for court to begin. He had gotten a call in the middle of the night from Alex that everything was done as he had instructed. Now, he just had to put the rest of his plan in motion. Craze looked down at a case containing fake passports and identification papers supplied by Mr. Odouwo for all of his crew members. There was also a get-away van that had previously been parked near the airport with diplomatic license plate tags. He lit up his blunt and waited for the Charlie's call as he looked at his watch. *It's about time we get us an ambulance ride*, he thought, imagining how sweet Dutch's getaway would be.

An ambulance had been called because of a report of a woman found unconscious in the parking lot behind the Newport Center Mall outside the Holland Tunnel. Two male EMTs rushed to the scene, sirens blaring. When the EMTs arrived the woman was down, lying still on the pavement. The two medics jumped out of the back of the van and rolled a stretcher over to the cataleptic woman. When one of the medics knelt to see if the woman was still breathing, his partner was shot in the back of the head at point-blank range.

"Holy shit!" the other medic shouted when he realized his partner had been killed.

"Get the fuck up!" the Charlie who was assumed to have been unconscious commanded as she put a gun to his head.

"Please don't kill me!" the EMT said, begging for his life, when the other Charlie pulled him up by the back of his shirt. "Call dispatch and tell them that the report was a false alarm and you'll get to live!" the Charlie informed him.

The medic got on the walkie-talkie and did just what he was told with a gun still pointed at his head.

"Dispatch, come in. Dispatch, come in!"

"This is dispatch, go ahead!"

"There was no one found at the scene behind the shopping mall! I repeat, there was no one found at the scene, over!"

"Copy that."

"Okay, it's done," the medic said after he was finished with the call.

"All right, now take off your clothes," one of the Charlies ordered.

"But it's cold outside."

"You want to live or you want to worry about the fucking weather?" said the Charlie, pointing the gun and ready to squeeze off.

While he quickly removed his clothes, the other Charlie stripped the dead EMT of his uniform. As soon as the Charlies had on the EMT uniforms, the half-naked medic was told to put his dead partner in the Dumpster. The medic used all his strength to sling his former partner into the huge waste fill.

"Now get your ass in there with him."

Fear overcame him as he slowly got into the awful-smelling trash container. One of the Charlies shot him in the chest before his feet even touched the bottom. She delivered two more shots to his frame to make sure he was dead. They both slammed down the top of the Dumpster, then headed to the courthouse.

Craze got the call letting him know the Charlies were on their way, sirens ready to blare. He hung up his phone while he twirled a brown triangle Branson bag between his fingers. His mind drifted as he reflected on everything that had been done in the past to get them to where they were today. He couldn't believe that they had moved from stealing cars, to controlling the streets of Newark, then to where they were now. This was the last chance for him to keep Dutch out of prison, and he hoped that he didn't fail his friend. After the blunt burned down to his fingertips Craze got out of the car and walked around to the back of the courthouse. He hid behind a Dumpster where he would wait until Dutch and the Charlies came through the back door blasting. *I know you gonna make it out of there. I just know you will.*

Dutch was given the floor so he could say his last words to the courtroom before the final verdict was read. He was to plead forgiveness, beg for mercy, and speak his last words of remorse. Instead, he got up out of his seat and said fuck you to everyone in the courtroom. He laughed and then flicked his lighter, which was the sign for the Charlies to come out with their guns blazing. Bullets flew loosely, killing everyone in plain view.

Dutch reached under the defense table and grabbed the two pistols that were waiting for him. He killed the judge and then killed District Attorney Anthony Jacobs. He looked through the aisles for Frank Bonno and found him curled up on the floor, before killing him, too, as officers stormed the courtroom firing shots at Dutch and the Charlies now surrounding him. Dutch watched one of his girls fall to the floor before letting off a couple of rounds.

"We got to get out of here. Now!" yelled one of the Charlies, leading the way, as she had the exit mapped out in her head.

"This way," she said, leading the pack, while some of the Charlies stayed behind to slow down the officers' pursuit.

The two Charlies who had stolen the ambulance were waiting along with Craze outside the back of the courthouse. Ever since they had heard the first shots being fired inside, Craze had sweated bullets.

"What the fuck is taking them so long?" he said as he listened to the gunfire being exchanged inside the courthouse, looking at his watch, keeping time.

Within minutes the four remaining Charlies ran out the back door with Dutch in tow. Craze watched as they got his man inside the ambulance. Once Dutch was safely tucked inside, Craze closed the doors and watched as the ambulance sirens came on and the van slipped out of all the commotion, passing right by the police. Craze walked over to his car, unnoticed. He walked right through the crowd of frightened people, media, and scattered police officers. He got into his car and drove away as if nothing had happened. It was that simple, and it was already done.

DEAD AT THE DOOR

The scene in front of the courthouse was chaotic as Craze drove past police cars and ambulances. He was laughing all the way home, knowing it was too late for the police to do a damn thing. And if everything went as planned, one of the Charlies would be setting a nice little fire inside the courthouse to add smoke to an already burning flame. Craze picked up his phone and called Mr. Odouwo.

"It's done," Craze said, smiling, letting him know Dutch had made it out of the courthouse.

Mr. Odouwo smiled back, as if the two men were face to face.

"Good. I will see you when you are done with your work here," Odouwo said before hanging up the phone and pouring himself a scotch, straight.

He picked up the phone again, dialing out to his personal assistant.

"Get me a flight to Paris right away," he commanded.

Mr. Odouwo finished his return calls for the day and took a sip from his drink as he sat back in a tall-backed alligator-skin chair behind his desk. He was exhaling deeply, clearing his lungs, sighing with relief. Life was moving the way he had planned. It had taken him some time, but he finally had all the pieces beginning to fit into place. Dutch, Frankie Bonno, the Mafia, all of them were merely pawns in his game. It was his move, and checkmate once again. He now had Dutch, and together they would accomplish what no one believed they could; power. He grinned a devilish grin, knowing all was falling into place. Soon he'd have everything there was in the world he could desire, everything.

Alex had been at the bar every night, buying drinks for everybody, playing pool, and having a good ol' time. He usually could only afford happy hour, but thanks to Craze and his first installment payment, he was on the road to riches and had no plans of detouring, until the news anchor lady showed up on the color monitor above his head at the bar.

"Hey, Joe, turn that up for me," said Alex as the husky Irishman turned up the television for Alex.

"You see this shit? Fucking asshole shot up the courtroom, killed the judge and the jury, every fucking body, they said," said Joe as Alex picked up his glass and set it down for Joe to fill back up.

"They killed everybody," murmured Alex, listening intently. He stared off in the distance, thinking of the role he had played in the deaths of all those innocent people. He had never thought about that, just the money. He had had no idea anyone would get hurt, let alone killed. *I'm a cold-blooded killer,* he thought to himself as he slung back another.

"Hey Alex, you all right over there, old fella?" asked the bartender, looking at the old sap sitting there. "Take it easy. Liquor ain't leaving."

Alex had never imagined that he would end up a contributor to murder. He should have known. What did he expect for a million dollars? His heart lay heavy as he watched the news reporter interviewing a husband whose wife was still inside. *He looks so sad, so worried.* He felt bad, now that he was able to see the damage that he had done. He wished he had never accepted the money or the offer. He ordered another round before leaving the bar and making his way home.

Just as he turned on the television, he heard a knock at his door.

He knew exactly who that was. *It's the police, that's who. Oh, my God, Jesus, Mother Mary, and Joseph, what am I going to do?* They were the last people on the face of the earth he wanted to see. His heart raced, and he was scared to answer the door. Quickly, he went over to his dresser and began grabbing extra clothing, some underwear, and the tiny box holding the Whitaker watch his dad had passed down to him. *Maybe the police will just go away and I can make a run for it.*

"Hey, Alex, open up, I know you're in there," said Craze from behind the door.

Oh thank God, he said, his heart feeling lighter at the thought of not being arrested and placed behind bars. He took a deep breath and walked slowly to the door. Craze knocked again as beads of sweat from Alex's brow trickled down the side of his face as he approached the door.

"Who is it?" he said faintly, looking out the peephole, making sure the police weren't behind the door setting him up.

"It's Craze! Open the door!"

Alex slowly pulled the door back, allowing Craze to enter his apartment. Alex hurried to shut the door behind him, after peeking around the door frame to make sure the coast was clear.

"What took you so long to answer the door? You act like you ain't tryna get paid," Craze said, holding Alex's bag of money up to him. "What the hell is wrong with you?" asked Craze, looking at Alex all sweaty, pupils dilated, his straggly wet hair sticking to the sides of his face.

"I thought you were the police."

"You expecting them?" asked Craze, wondering why he was even speaking of them.

"After what happened today in the courthouse, I'm hoping not," said Alex as he paced the floor. "I can't believe you used me like that to kill all those people. The news said sixty-seven people were injured and forty-two people were killed. What the fuck am I supposed to do now?"

Craze looked at Alex as if he was bugging. "What are you talking about? Man, what the fuck is you on in here? I suggest you take this money and go somewhere tropical, forget your life, start a new one." Craze smiled, not realizing that the alcohol had given Alex what some folks referred to as the "rams" and Alex was ready to pick a fight. Only problem was, he was picking it with the wrong person.

"What am I supposed to do now?"

"Whatever the fuck you want! Why in the hell are you sweating?" Craze asked, realizing that while Alex had done the job well, he was now blowing a tiny situation out of proportion. "You scared or something, Alex?" asked Craze, chuckling at Alex's frazzled appearance.

"I want you to get the hell out of here. Shit, I wouldn't be surprised if the police show up here any minute," he said, moving his hands and shaking his head. "I can't believe what I've gotten myself into. What in the world was I thinking?" he asked himself as he stared off into the distance.

"Yo, Alex, you bugging, man, be easy."

"I don't think you understand. You just shot up an entire courthouse full of innocent people and then set it on fire and burned it down," he said as he walked a few steps away from Craze.

"I should have never done it. What in God's name was I thinking? All those poor people?"

Craze smiled and drew his gun, pointing it at Alex.

"You know what, Alex?"

"No, I don't know," he said, shaking his head "no" as if he really didn't, still unaware of the cold steel barrel pointed at him from behind, across the floor.

"Since you can't handle seemingly tiny situations and you want to act like a fucking girl and shit, I think we're gonna have to stop here and cut our ties, okay, pal? But you did good, though, Alex, real good."

Craze had really thought Alex could stand up under pressure, but he couldn't. Alex screamed in fear as he realized Craze's gun was pointed at him. He took two shots to the chest, silencing his plea as Craze sent him to meet his maker. Then Craze shot him once more in the back of his head, guaranteeing death. Craze laughed as he left Alex's body on the floor. "Wow, this gots to be the dumbest motherfucker I ever met in my life," said Craze, tucking his gun inside the waist of his pants. He picked up the briefcase and walked out of the apartment holding a cool million, another job well done.

Detectives would of course be investigating all those who

had access to the courthouse. Alex Kelly's name would cross a desk or two, but not until he had failed to show up for work three nights in row. Unfortunately, when the detectives finally showed up at his door, they would find his dead body on the floor. The death of the courthouse janitor was all the evidence they would need to link Alex to the plot. And when they found the manila envelope filled with hundred-dollar bills, that was all the evidence they would need that he had been a part of Dutch's murderous escape plan.

FLY ME TO THE MOON

Dutch watched as the Charlies quickly changed from their grandma attire into black leather catsuits in the back of the ambulance that had conveniently transported them from the courthouse. A van with diplomatic plates, courtesy of Mr. Odouwo, had been parked and was waiting for them. They left the ambulance in the van's spot and headed straight to Newark Airport. They arrived at the airport and boarded a private plane headed to Paris's Charles de Gaulle Airport. Dutch figured since Newark Airport was the closest, it was the quickest and safest route out of the country. It was surely their best chance to escape. Odouwo had prearranged a private passenger carrier under the names on the phony passports. All they had to do was get to the private passenger plane before the police realized Dutch was missing from the courthouse. The plane was ready and waiting when they arrived. There were no checkpoints, ticketing, or security measures used when traveling by private jet. They boarded the plane and no one suspected a thing.

Once they were in Paris, a limo was waiting to take them to Hôtel de Crillon. Shortly after checking in, Dutch got a call from Mr. Odouwo.

"I see you made it safely. All is well?" asked Odouwo.

"All is very well, thank you," responded Dutch.

The two men spoke briefly and Odouwo assured Dutch he would be landing shortly. Within a matter of hours, Mr. Odouwo and two of his henchmen knocked on the door of Dutch's Louis XV suite. One of the Charlies answered the door and allowed Mr. Odouwo to enter. She led Odouwo into the foyer, down a long narrow hallway to two double doors where Dutch was waiting.

Upon Odouwo's entering the room, Dutch politely stood to greet him, extending his hand and shaking Odouwo's.

"Mr. Bernard James. It's a pleasure to finally meet you," Mr. Odouwo said, smiling and still holding Dutch's hand in his.

"No, I think the pleasure is mine," Dutch said, thinking of the torture he would have faced had he been sentenced to life behind bars.

"On many levels I would have to disagree with you, Mr. James. You are the one with the more interesting life story of the two of us. You just pulled off the biggest escape in history. From what I hear, you are on every news station in America. Yours is a story that has the nation in awe. I was just watching Anderson Cooper. I don't think you understand: This is an amazing triumph, my friend. They are calling you 'America's Most Wanted,' yes?"

Dutch smiled. "From what I hear from your old Mafia

cronies, you had some successful escapes yourself," Dutch said, referring to the mob's failed attempts on his life.

"That was just bad strategy on their part, Mr. James. If you were after me, I would be dead, I'm sure, just as my nephew Kazami is right now, wouldn't you agree?"

Dutch avoided answering the question, even though he knew the answer and so did Odouwo.

"I guess we'll never know now, will we?" Dutch said.

"No, I'm most confident we won't," Mr. Odouwo said, shaking his head and hoping that Dutch would never betray him, after all he had done to see the man free.

Mr. Odouwo stared into Dutch's eyes, dark brown, just like his own, before continuing.

"Mr. James. I would like you and your friends to accompany me for dinner so we can discuss business. Meet me at the hotel restaurant in two hours. Reservations will be under my name."

Dutch agreed, and Mr. Odouwo nodded and headed for the door. Dutch walked out on the balcony and looked into the approaching Paris night. He knew he was far away from home and was farther away from jail. He smiled, knowing that he had been given a new start. And a new start was exactly what it was, a new chance to make his mark even bigger than it already was.

Dutch and the Charlies, with not much packed in their suitcases, under the circumstances, went out for a quick shopping spree on Avenue Montaigne and the Champs-Élysées. The girls bought dresses, Dutch a three-piece suit, and while he didn't have time to have it fitted, it actually lay against him perfectly. They arrived at the restaurant with only a few minutes to spare and were ushered inside by a valet. Before Dutch could tell the maître d' his party's name, he was quickly escorted over to Mr. Odouwo, who was already seated and waiting patiently.

"Mr. James. I see you're right on time," Mr. Odouwo said as he stood to greet Dutch.

"That's the only way to be," Dutch said, smiling as he took his seat.

"I couldn't agree more. I think the waiter needs to be right on time as well—I'm starving," Mr. Odouwo joked.

After dinner, but before dessert and coffee, Mr. Odouwo thought it would be a good time to discuss business.

"Mr. James. Let's take a walk." They got up and walked through the restaurant to the outside terrace on the roof with its view of the Eiffel Tower.

"So, I take it your friend explained to you why you're here?" Mr. Odouwo asked, giving Dutch a glance.

"It basically boils down to you wantin' murder for diamonds."

"Did he tell you who I want you to kill?"

"I told him it didn't matter as long as I got out."

"Interesting," said Odouwo, squinting at Dutch, realizing just how ruthless the man before him really was. "But if you don't mind, I'd like to tell you who the person is anyway."

Dutch shrugged, letting Mr. Odouwo know he didn't mind listening.

"Your target is Taji Tita. He's the president of Nigeria," said Odouwo. "Is that still not a problem for you?" Mr. Odouwo looked at Dutch, trying to see if there was any uncertainty in his eyes, but there wasn't. Mr. Odouwo knew then that there was nothing that could change Dutch's mind. He was a stone-cold killer.

"Nope, never heard of the man. Listen, Mr. Odouwo, let me be real clear with you so no one is confused. My one and only concern is how do my team and I benefit from all this?" Dutch asked.

"Do you mean besides your freedom?" Mr. Odouwo smiled sarcastically. Dutch, unfortunately, was unable to find any humor in the man's words. "Mr. James, I can make you and your friends very wealthy. I'm talking about the kind of wealth that makes all the money you ever made amount to chickenshit. I'm talking about these."

Mr. Odouwo held up a diamond so big and dazzling that it made Dutch's eyes convulse. It was a beautiful stone, the most beautiful Dutch had ever seen. Mr. Odouwo noticed the zealous expression that came over Dutch's face and knew it wouldn't be hard to make him happy.

"So, Mr. James, I take it you like what you see?" asked Odouwo as he extended his hand, the diamond resting neatly in his palm. "Well, if that is the case, you can have it."

Mr. Odouwo tossed the oversized gem to Dutch without warning. Dutch caught the diamond in midair.

"I don't know if I should take it without knowing what it's worth to you," Dutch said, knowing that everything of merit had a price. He held his new best friend up in the air. "She's beautiful. Damn, look at that sparkle." Dutch smiled, still waiting to hear its worth.

"A dollar, that's what it was worth before it was mined. Now it's worth millions. Tomorrow I'll take you to see the mines, diamonds worth five million dollars and more. You can just imagine how much they'll go for on the market. You keep that, a little token of what's yet to come."

Mr. Odouwo checked his watch. "Let's get back to our guests. We don't want to be rude now, do we? We can pick back up on this tomorrow. Now, we'll enjoy our evening together."

Dutch and Mr. Odouwo walked back into the restaurant with a clearer understanding of each other.

The next morning they took a private jet to Sierra Leone. They arrived in Freetown International Airport where a car was waiting for them. Dutch had never been to Africa. It was vast, beautiful, and breathtaking. He looked out the window at the West African landscape. The sun was dancing across mother earth, leaving a bright glow of orange. It was the most beautiful landscape he'd ever seen in his life, even more beautiful than the Amazon rainforest. They approached a swampy area between hills, where dozens of child slaves toddled through the murky water, as armed soldiers held their posts.

"I love to see my children working," Mr. Odouwo said proudly as they drove by them.

The car finally stopped at the entrance of a cave where the old and the young were being put to work, mining the diamonds. Mr. Odouwo wanted Dutch to get out of the car and see the mining effort for himself. When they neared the entrance of the cave, Mr. Odouwo called over to one of the boys, asking to see what he had pulled from the cave. The young boy opened his sack so Mr. Odouwo could see inside it. Mr. Odouwo smiled as he pulled out a large stone and held it up in the air.

"See, I told you I would have some for five dollars," Mr. Odouwo said, showing Dutch the mud-covered stone.

The diamond was three times bigger than the one Mr. Odouwo had given him last night, even though Dutch couldn't imagine them being any bigger. And now that Dutch saw the entire operation up close, he was even more intrigued by the thought of working with Mr. Odouwo.

"So, do you like what you see so far?" Mr. Odouwo asked with a big smile on his face.

"Yeah, this is serious. I definitely want a part of this."

"How did I know you were going to say that? Now come, I have to take you to meet my uncle."

They boarded the plane, and the captain took them to Abuja, Nigeria. Abuja, the capital of Nigeria, was Odouwo's hometown and the place where he had grown from a boy to a man. As they drove down the dirt road into the city, Mr. Odouwo swanked about his beautiful country.

"Aww, Nigeria. There's nothing else like it. It's the most beautiful country in the world. Look at the trees, look at the land, and look at the people. Sorry Frank Sorbonno never got a chance to see what I was talking about." Mr. Odouwo snickered while thinking about how he had set Frank up to be killed.

"Yeah, Frank would have loved it," Dutch said, returning the sarcasm.

Not too far from the city limits, they pulled up to a large gated estate. Once they entered the compound, they could see Mr. Odouwo's uncle, Yusef Odouwo, standing on the front lawn holding a baby tiger. Yusef was an older version of Mr. Odouwo, apart from his bald head and slender frame. Judging by his style, Dutch could tell he had just as much influence as Mr. Odouwo had or more. They got out of the car and walked toward Yusef as he walked toward them.

"How are you, my nephew?" Yusef said in his Igbo accent, glad to see him.

"Now that I'm home I feel wonderful." They shook hands, and Mr. Odouwo rested his other hand on Yusef's shoulder. "Uncle, it's been a long time."

"Yes, Joseph, it has. The days grow shorter as you get older," said the wise older man.

"Uncle, you're finally admitting to getting older, are you?"

"No, nephew, I was referring to you. You are getting old. We just saw each other two months ago."

"Being away from home more than a week seems like a lifetime."

"I understand what you mean." They shared a laugh.

"Uncle, I would like you to meet a friend of mine," Mr. Odouwo said, looking at Dutch.

"So, I take it you are Mr. James, am I correct?"

"I am. It's nice to meet you."

"Mr. James, that is yet to be seen, I haven't had lunch yet. I can get very angry without food in my stomach," Yusef said, joking. "Come. Let's talk more inside," he added, inviting them into his quarters.

On the back patio a magnificent array of food was waiting for them on the gathering table. After the meal, they were all ready to talk about business.

"So, Mr. James, how are you liking Nigeria so far?" Yusef asked.

"I've never been to Africa, so the whole experience is mind-blowing."

"The whole experience, you say?" Yusef questioned.

"I took them to the diamond field this morning," Mr. Odouwo explained.

"Aww, diamonds. That is an interesting experience, to see the diamonds being mined from out of mother earth. It's crazy to think that something so lucid and precious can come from a piece of dirty coal. It's sort of like the whole triumph of the black man. Any of us can come from unforgiving conditions and turn them around into something grand."

Dutch knew all about coming from the bottom, coming from nothing with a foot in his back. His whole life had been built around compromise until he took things into his own hands. Now he was considered impressive not only by himself but by many others.

"Mr. James. I don't trust many men, but after looking into your eyes I can tell you are more a man of action than of words. And when I look at you, I see no fear. Is there anything you fear, Mr. James?" asked Yusef.

"I wouldn't call it a fear, but the only thing I will avoid at all cost is going back to prison."

"I hear prison is a very terrible place. I wouldn't want to go there either. The only thing I will avoid at all cost is being poor again. I think we can both help each other."

"I believe we can, too," Dutch responded, ready to get down to business. He understood where Yusef was coming from and planned to give him any assistance he needed.

"Now that we have that out of the way, let me tell you about our dilemma."

Dutch was more than eager to listen.

"Taji Tita has made it illegal for the citizens of Nigeria, Uganda, and Rwanda to lease diamond fields. He doesn't understand how the resources from diamonds can benefit our people, if our people had control of them, yet he commends surrounding countries for their successful diamond networks. We want to shut all those networks down and ultimately control Africa's entire diamond trade, as we should. This is where you come in, Mr. James. French oil billionaire Kelsin Borvalo is having a party in Paris a week from now, and Tita is invited. And if you're wondering how we are sure that Tita will attend, trust that I know," said Yusef, sitting down and crossing his legs like a woman. He sipped his cocktail, then nodded at Dutch, "Tita granted Borvalo a monopoly deal to export oil from Nigeria. This is another reason why we don't respect Tita as president. Things need to change in Nigeria and the other countries for our people, but with Tita in office that can't happen. We can't wait any longer for a new day in Nigeria. It has to be certain that Tita doesn't leave that party. Can that be achieved, Mr. James?" he asked.

"Consider it done," Dutch responded, expressionless.

He understood the extent of what was being asked of him, and he was more than willing to comply. President Tita had no relevance to Dutch, and if his demise would bring Dutch closer to fulfilling his financial destiny, then that man's life was a small price to pay. After they had all sat and talked shop for a while longer, Yusef finished sealing the deal and etching out their plans for how Tita would be assassinated. When the meeting was finished, Mr. Odouwo and Dutch got on the plane and headed back to Paris, the wheels already set in motion.

DEAD OR ALIVE

Newark, New Jersey

Delores hadn't gone to the courthouse. Instead, she sat patiently in front of the television glued to Fox 5 News watching and waiting as the reporters kept showing live updates of what was happening at the courthouse. Then she got the call. She'd never forget how fast they showed up at her door to take her down to the city's morgue to identify her son. She couldn't imagine him not being a part of the world that she was in. She couldn't imagine not hearing his voice again, not touching his face again, and never holding him in her arms. No mother wants to outlive her child, but having to identify a dead body belonging to your only son, now that was something else. And as horrendous and stressful as the day had already been, she couldn't imagine seeing him lying dead on that table. But she agreed, and within the hour was standing inside the County Coroner's Office, a detective on either side of her.

They placed her in a room that seemed completely sterilized. A body was lying on the table in front of her, covered with a white sheet. Detective Meritti explained everything that had transpired before her son's death, before the fire trapped him inside the courthouse, bringing him to his untimely demise. Detective Meritti showed her a set of matching dental records before placing the folder at the foot of the table. He slowly went to the head of the table and lifted the sheet for her to view the body and make a positive ID. Delores looked down at the body before her. *I don't know who the hell these police officers think they got lying on this table, but this ain't no damn son of mine, that's for sure.*

"Oh, God, no, please no, not my baby," she said, beginning an award performance as she claimed the body as being that of Dutch.

Wait till I get hold of him. He ain't even dead. And now he got me burying God only knows who. I swear I'm gonna kill that boy if it's the last thing I do.

"It's okay, ma'am, we're here," said Meritti reassuringly as he moved the distraught mother away from the table and out of the room. "She's made a positive over here. Can I get a cup of water? She's a little distraught," said Detective Smalls.

Delores acted her ass off, completely relieved that Dutch was not on that table. Yet, if you didn't know better, from the way she was acting, you would think she had lost her only begotten son. Detective Smalls studied Delores's emotions, waiting to see how she would react to the body they were presenting as that of her son. Apparently, to him, and to everyone else watching, she was buying it. *She's too distraught, the tears, the look in her eyes. She's going to sign for the body, thank God.* Delores continued to perform her Academy Award–winning role as a grieving mother, all the while playing them like a fiddle.

Delores stood in the hallway trying to figure out what in the world was going on, all the while she continued to break down and cry as if that was really her son. She wore the mask well. The pain that the detectives saw in her eyes wasn't from the belief that her son was dead, but because he was still alive. Delores was now more confused and flooded with emotion than she had been when they first lifted the sheet. But her tears were truly tears of joy. Even though she knew the reign of terror that would come from this, and that the nightmare was nowhere near over. Delores signed her name, accepting the body of the imposter they wanted her to believe was Dutch. *Whoever the hell he is, I'ma go ahead and bury him. No, wait, cremation is so much cheaper. Yeah, I'll let the funeral director know we'll have a service then we'll go that route.* Delores figured she could have the body cremated so that Dutch's secret could be scattered to the winds, never to be questioned again.

When Delores left the detectives, of course she was followed, and of course her phones were tapped. The police knew that the body they had presented wasn't Dutch's. They only placed the dead body in front of her for the media's sake and for their own reputations. Honestly, they figured eventually everyone reaches out for their momma, and Delores already knew it. She was one step ahead of them all the way around the mulberry bush. And she already knew they would do everything in their power to try to use her to get to Dutch, from tapping her phone lines to constant surveillance. It didn't matter. She was one step ahead of them.

CAN'T STOP, WON'T STOP

Paris, France

Craze arrived in Paris after he had finished his business and tied up all the loose ends in Newark. He was finally going to get a chance to celebrate Dutch's great escape. Craze had been friends with Dutch as long as he could remember. Their parents were good friends when they were young, and it wasn't a surprise that they were best friends now, more like brothers, actually. Craze thought back on the days when they first started hanging and getting into trouble together, when he had been known merely as Chris.

Chris's mother died of a brain aneurysm when he was eight. He had to go live with his aunt, and from that day on he wasn't the same sweet child everyone knew so well. He had loved had his mother so much, and he felt like his whole world was lost without her. Even though he had an aunt who would do anything for him, there was still nothing like having his mother, and he missed her terribly.

"Watch this," Chris said to Dutch as they stood on the rooftop of his high-rise building.

A squad car was making its rounds and Chris was just waiting for it to get in the right spot. When it did, he launched a piece of a brick over the side and watched it crash into the police car's window. Chris and Dutch started laughing, until the police officer stepped out of the car and looked up at them. They both ran into the building and laughed all day about what had happened. This was just the beginning of Chris and Dutch's friendship. It would last throughout their childhood and all their adult lives.

"Hey, girl, what's ya name?" Chris asked, stopping a young Catholic school girl as she walked home with her friend.

"Joy. What's yours?" she asked.

"My name's Chris, and this here is my main man Dutch. He's a crazy motherfucker. He just killed a cop the other day. Right down the street."

Dutch just shook his head and laughed, wondering why Craze always told kids far-fetched stories about him. Neither of them had any idea at the time that they would really grow up and knock off the Police Department, or at least try, every chance they got. But they did, and the history between the two was all Craze had of memories. It was hard to remember his own momma without looking at her picture, but Dutch, he had memories of the two of them to fill the pages of a book.

Dutch watched Craze coax the girls to follow them up on the rooftop where they could have their way under the stars. Craze always said that the girls liked the romantic stuff. And the rooftop was the perfect place.

"See, look, right there, that's the Big Dipper, and over there is the Little Dipper," said Craze, not knowing what the hell he was pointing at. The girls would fall for it, every time. That's how it was, Craze didn't have much of a family, but he had Dutch, and they came up together, doing everything under the sun together. From getting pussy in mulberry bushes to going to Sunday church with Ms. Delores, they had done everything together and they still did. They always would.

By the time Chris turned twelve he had shed his childish layers and was on his way to becoming a young man. He and Dutch would only go to school half of the time while they spent the other half causing havoc, letting their names be heard around the neighborhood. Chris would bully kids in school, stomping their asses out in the schoolyard if they didn't comply with his demands. He did this just to hold Dutch's attention or because Dutch had beef with someone.

Everybody knew Chris was crazy. Most people saw him coming and went the other way. It had become a nickname of sorts—because of his antics, everyone started calling him Crazy Chris, which over time shortened into Craze. The more people knew he was not playing with a full deck of cards, the more the nickname stuck. Like Dutch, Craze refused to let anyone play him like a sucker. The first person who tried had to learn shit the hard way.

Craze was tagging his name on a wall in the alleyway behind a corner store with a can of black spray paint. Dutch was supposed to bring the red spray but wasn't there yet. Craze was in such a rush to get his name up for everyone to see, he decided to start without him. He sprayed on a big *C* and then a lowercase *r*. He was about to spray on the letter *a*, but he heard a group of kids come up behind him.

"Yo, muthafucka. What you doin' taggin' on our turf?" the biggest of the three boys said.

Craze looked at him like he was stupid. "Your turf? Nigga, me and my nigga run all this shit 'round here. I'm Craze, and I know you heard of my man Dutch. So if y'all pussies know what's good for ya you'll turn and get the fuck outta here while you still got the chance, ya hear?"

"Yo, son, I'm gonna wear ya lil' ass out."

The boy ran up, and Craze dropped his can and rose to his feet. As the boy rushed him, Craze moved out of the way and caught him with a blow to his eye. Before the boy could make another move Craze caught him with a blind left, knocking him to the ground.

One of the other boys ran up behind Craze and tried to hold him until his friend got up off the ground. Craze was stronger than he looked, and he was able to get out of the hold he was in. He punched the boy in the stomach and then pushed him into the wall. The boy got Craze in a headlock and the other two boys jumped on him, beating him down in the street.

Out of nowhere Dutch came up from behind and swung a right so hard, so fast, he dropped one of the boys with a single blow. Dutch fought off another boy, giving him an uppercut to the kidneys and careening him into a dumpster. Craze picked up the boy who was choking him, flipped him over his shoulder, and began to stomp him out while Dutch beat the one boy up so bad that both his eyes would be swollen for a week. After that, Craze and Dutch became household names. Their popularity grew as well as their menacing ways, and then along came murder.

Craze sat in his bedroom leaning out his window smoking a cigarette one night when he heard Dutch's bird call from outside his window.

"Yo! Come here! I gotta show you somethin'," Dutch hollered.

Craze came down the fire escape and was standing in front of Dutch in a matter of seconds.

"What up?" Craze asked.

"Just come on."

They walked around the corner and Craze saw a white van sitting halfway down the block. Dutch thought the van he'd stolen belonged to his boss, the guy who owned the pizza shop, but he didn't know it was deeper than that.

"Yo, Craze, I love you like a brother, but once I open this door and show you what's inside, ain't no turning back, nigga. You either wit' me or go on and walk away now," Dutch solemnly declared.

Craze looked Dutch in the eye. He had never heard such words from him before. Dutch was all he had, and he would die for him or even die with him if it came down to it. He knew what Dutch had to show him was serious. Nothing like he had ever seen before. Craze was ready.

"Yo, Duke, you know how we get down. You and I, do or die—you ain't got to tell me to walk nowhere," Craze stated.

Dutch looked him in the eyes and when he was satisfied he nodded and opened the back doors of the van. Craze stepped up to the van and saw a long, bulky object between two garbage bags. Dutch snatched off one of the garbage bags to reveal the dead body. Craze took one look and threw up all inside the van.

"Damn, nigga! We got enough to clean up wit'out yo ass addin' to it!" Dutch said.

"What the fuck happened to him?" Craze asked after he'd emptied his stomach.

"Never mind, we need a whole lot of cinderblocks and some rope," Dutch responded.

Craze asked no more questions that night, and when it was all said and done, there was no turning back. It was him and Dutch, thick as thieves, and the bond they shared from that night on would keep them together for the rest of their lives. As time passed, the bond would only become stronger and stronger, unbreakable. No matter where they were in the world, from Newark to Paris, it didn't matter. Dutch was the only family Craze had, the only family he remembered ever having all his life. For him, Dutch was his brother, and he was his brother's keeper; he always would be.

After wrapping everything up back in Newark, Craze landed in Paris's Charles de Gaulle Airport and took a taxi to the hotel. He opened the double doors to his presidential suite. He dropped his carry-on next to the bed. He couldn't believe it, all the planning and scheming had paid off. How they did it put a smile on his face. He opened the French doors to the balcony. He looked out into the Paris sky, the city twinkling below him. The balcony he stood on had been occupied by kings and queens, who had once reigned from it. It made him think back to how it all started. They had dared to do the impossible and they had made it look easy. They had taken on any and all, meeting every challenge and winning them all. He held up an issue of *Don Diva* magazine. "Is Dutch Really Dead" was the caption. He stared at a photograph of Roc as the door to the suite opened and closed. He walked back into the room to greet the three surviving Charlies, accompanied by the man he had walked through hell with and emerged on the other side with, unscathed.

Dutch.

Craze handed Dutch the magazine. He looked at the picture of Roc on the cover.

"Even Roc thinks you're dead," Craze said as he pulled out a cigarette and checked his pockets for a light. Dutch pulled out the lighter he had taken from Mrs. Piazza. It was the same lighter he used to signal the Charlies at the trial.

He held it up while Craze lit his cigarette from it. Craze blew out a smoke ring as Dutch replied. "They can't stop what they can't see."

"Shit, these motherfuckers can't stop what they can see. Can't stop, won't stop, baby," said Craze, giving Dutch a pound and a manly embrace. They were together at last, their plan a success. After all they had been through, it was now a new day.

"It's good to see you, fam. Welcome to Paris," Dutch said, hugging his best man in the entire world.

"Good to see you, too. It's good to see all of you," Craze said, embracing the three remaining Charlies. "I wish we would have all made it though," he added, thinking about all the Charlies lost in the courtroom.

"Yeah, me, too. They died for me and they will always be in my memory. They would want our mission to continue."

"So what's next for us?" Craze asked.

"The president of Nigeria doesn't arrive here for another week, but he's next on our agenda."

"Well, what do we do until then?"

"We act normal as possible. We simply blend in."

"Well, if we're going to do that I need to see what Paris is all about. I think it's time we did something to celebrate your escape."

"What did you have in mind?"

Craze gave a devilish smile, letting Dutch know he need not ask but merely enjoy the ride.

Of course, Craze had them in what one might call a brothel,

full of beautiful, full-bodied French women. They were there to never say no, whatever you wanted, whatever you desired, whatever you craved, you would be sexually satisfied, orally, anally, two women, one woman, S&M, whatever you wanted, even costumes, rooms complete with ropes, dancing poles, and everything one needed to really get one's freak on.

"Damn, you see them, I don't know who to pick, they all look so amazing," said Craze, greedily picking five to have his way with. "I'm fucking all of them."

But not Dutch. Dutch picked but one, beautiful, petite, perfectly shaped, sexy, with long dark brown hair, possibly Venezuelan, maybe Portuguese, olive-toned, soft, and willing to do what he commanded, anything he commanded. And when he was finished having her, she would be dismissed and he would pick another, if he wished, but never the same chick twice. No, he wanted to pick and discard, to have the next one in line, and the others waiting for his return, waiting to be chosen by him again. For him this was much more satisfying, and to have them all be willing participants in his escapade made it an even better ride, no secrets, no games. That's how he liked it. He would enjoy Paris, and the women in it.

Besides doing women, they did the streets, every night and every day, until they learned Paris and the cities surrounding it. He loved Paris, the city of love. It was where romance blossomed, and he enjoyed the energy, the fondling, kissing, groping, and constant display of affection, wherever or whenever. He enjoyed watching the people, their romance and their love on open display. Craze couldn't stay out of the night clubs. They became an aphrodisiac and he partied like a rock star. Sex, drugs, lights, camera, action, Paris had it all, and Craze devoured everything the city had to offer.

The only thing missing in Paris was Nina. Every now and then for a split second she would creep into the depths of Dutch's memory bank. Her beautiful, soft, brown skin, and long silky hair, he never let go, not completely. She was the one who got away, the one he deeply desired. She was the one who refused him. The one he couldn't control, put in line, and she wasn't the one waiting. He thought about her, wondering if she thought he was dead, wondering if she yearned for him or had put her feelings to rest and moved on. He thought of her quite often. He often wondered if he had made a mistake not including her or telling her his plan to escape. But he knew he had done the right thing. The level of trust that it would take for him to confide in a woman was something he often wondered if he'd ever find. For him, trust outweighed love, likewise respect. Had he shared one detail of his plans to escape with her he would never have slept at night. He simply decided to do what needed to be done, still keeping a distant eye until it was the right time and the right place for them to reunite. At the same time, he was working on a way to contact his mother. He figured the police had to know by now that he was alive, that he had survived and somehow gotten away, despite the funeral held for him or whoever his mother had signed for. He wondered if his mother knew he was okay. *She knows I'm good. She has to know that wasn't me; she's my mother. If she don't know, who else would?* It was too hard to contact her at the present, but the time would soon come when he would beckon her as well.

GROOVE LINE

President Tita walked into Kelsin Borvalo's extravagant gala heavily guarded by his loyal officers. Tita stepped through double doors and entered the dining hall and dance floor wearing a custom-made Bohemian suit draped with the finest of twenty-four-karat gold accessories. Tita was a short man, but he had the ego of a giant. He walked into the party head held high, knowing he would be the center of attention—partly because of his large entourage.

Mr. Odouwo had figured Tita would be hard to get close to as he was surrounded by his small army at all times. So plan number one was to use one of the Charlies in hopes of getting the president's attention. The president was known for having a weakness for beautiful American women, and any of the Charlies would surely qualify, as desirable as they were, but especially Dutch's favorite, Clair.

Clair was beautiful and enchanting and had glamour and

appeal that lured men to her. Yet her desire wasn't for men; it was for women. However, if Dutch needed her to play that role, it would be done. Clair turned up at the function wearing a Lagerfeld strapless gown with Louboutin sandals. She strolled through the double doors and entered the dining hall and dance floor, her eyes casing everything and everyone until she found her counterparts, the two other Charlies there to back her up. Once she made contact with her people, she set her sights on Tita and began to search for him through the crowd.

Mr. Odouwo made his appearance shortly after Clair did, with a mob of henchmen in tow. Mr. Odouwo was also an acquaintance of Kelsin Borvalo, through ties he had in the oil-exporting business. Those ties were the ones who had made sure Tita was invited to tonight's gala.

"Clair, how are you?" said Odouwo, leaning forward in a greeting.

"Oh, I'm fine. I'm just looking around—never know who you will find," she joked, still not spotting Tita.

"He's right behind you. Actually he's looking straight at us, so hopefully he'll catch the bait," Mr. Odouwo said, whispering into her ear.

"Oh, he's going to catch more than that," Clair responded, sweeping her hair from her face. They both laughed and sipped from their champagne glasses.

Moments later, one of the president's guards wearing a formal uniform approached Mr. Odouwo.

"Excusez-moi, monsieur. Le Président Tita aimerait parler avec vous," the guard informed him.

"Thank you very much," Mr. Odouwo said, nodding to him as he turned and smiled at Clair. Mr. Odouwo followed the guard back over to the Tita, the wheels beginning to turn.

"Mr. President, how are you?" Mr. Odouwo asked, smiling a radiant and exuberant smile. He did more than that; he turned on the big C—charm.

"I'm watching this lovely woman you have with you this evening." He smiled, knowing damn well she wasn't no Mrs. Odouwo. "Do you mind telling me who she is?"

Mr. Odouwo smiled, knowing that he was about to have Tita eating out of the palm of his hand.

"I would be delighted to make your introduction. Her name is Clair Washington. She's American, but is over in Dubai working for the Nations Trust financial institution based in Cape Town. She's brokered a few deals for me, actually. She's a very smart woman."

"Yes, I'd love to meet her," said Tita, smiling like an old man with new dentures as he looked across the room where Odouwo had asked Clair to wait.

Mr. Odouwo leaned over to Tita and put a bug in his ear.

"Mr. President. I have to warn you. Ms. Washington is a very aggressive woman, attracted to very powerful men," Mr. Odouwo said, giving him a wink.

"Oh, you don't say?" Tita said, becoming even more interested in her, knowing his influential stature fit the bill.

"Would you mind asking her if she would like to join me for a drink?" Tita asked.

"It would be my pleasure, Mr. President."

"Thank you. I owe you many favors for this," Tita said, showing his gratitude.

Mr. Odouwo smiled and quickly walked over to where Clair was standing.

"It worked. He wants to have a drink with you." Odouwo smiled.

Clair made eye contact with the president, smiled willingly, and nodded at him across the floor.

"I will make the introduction and signal Dutch that everything is going as planned."

He walked over and made the introduction, then quickly looked at his cell phone as if there were trouble.

"Is everything all right?" asked Tita.

"Oh, yes, Mr. President, I just need to step away for one second. Please forgive me for being so rude."

"No, no, your manners have been most appropriate. Go ahead, make your call, I will take care of Ms. Washington," he said as he turned his attention to Clair.

"It's very nice to meet you, Mr. President," Clair said, smiling from ear to ear.

"No, please. Call me Taji, and the pleasure is mine. What are you drinking tonight?"

"Champagne, thank you."

"Coming right up," Tita said, turning to one of his guards and asking for two glasses of the Cristal that the servers were carrying around on sterling silver trays.

"Here you are," Tita said, handing her a glass.

"Thank you."

"And a toast?"

"Why of course. What would we be toasting to?"

"How about to a glorious evening of the two of us making each other's acquaintance," Tita said, raising his glass and watching closely for her response.

"Yes, to us...getting," she said smoothly batting her eyelashes at him, "shall we say...acquainted," she added shifting her weight from side to side before touching his flute with hers.

They each took a sip, as Tita imagined her naked body. He was at a loss for words and unable to take his eyes off her.

"You know, Taji? You have a seductive smile, very, very, sexy. I'm sure all you do is smile and women are attracted to you like bees to honey."

"Thank you, but I think you are the more seductive and sexy of the two of us," he said, starting to get his composure back.

She looked at him, sipped champagne, parted her mouth half open and licked her lips with her tongue seductively.

"Would you like to go somewhere private, where we could be alone and I could really make your acquaintance?" he asked, already knowing she'd say yes.

"Yes, of course, how can I refuse?"

"Follow my security. I will make a few more greetings and meet you on the top floor. There is a conference room next to the penthouse suite."

She willingly followed two of Tita's security officers, who led her out the double doors of the dining area and down the hall to the elevators. She watched carefully as the officer to her right pressed the P button on the elevator, indicating that they were going to the penthouse suite. *Perfect*, she thought to herself. *Everything is going just like Dutch planned it.* The elevator doors opened and Clair could see the double doors of the penthouse suite a few feet down the hall.

"This way," said one of the security officers, leading Clair away from the penthouse.

"But... I, um, I thought I was waiting for Tita in his suite?" she questioned, wondering why they were leading her in the opposite direction.

"The president has requested that you wait for him in the conference lounge," answered the officer as he opened the door to the conference hall. There was a private conference room the president could hold formal meetings in. A sitting area, equipped with flat-screen TV, sofas, and chairs. On the other side of the room was a bar where a waiter could order anything from alcoholic beverages to chicken paninis. It was in itself a clubhouse of sorts where the president could entertain. After the guards made a clean sweep of the conference hall rooms, the waiter, and finally Clair to make sure she wasn't concealing any weapons, Tita was escorted into the conference room alongside two other security officers.

"*Tout va bien ici?*" he questioned.

"*Oui, monsieur, nous avons vérifié chaque pouce carrée.*"

"*Merveilleux. Quittez-nous,*" he ordered, watching as the four security officers walked out of the room, closing the door behind them.

This was nothing new for the guards, to find places for Tita to have sex with women. They would just wait outside the conference room door until Tita was finished.

Inside, Tita watched as Clair lay on top of the conference table and spread her legs slightly. She watched as Tita loosened his tie, unbuttoned a few buttons of his Loro Piana dress shirt and walked over to her, bent down on top of her, and began kissing her as she finished unbuttoning his shirt. Tita rolled on top of her, pressing his package firmly against her. She could feel his rock-hard penis through his clothing as his hand slid up her dress.

"What are you waiting for?" she moaned as she removed his tie, pulling it over his head.

Excited, Tita got up and dropped his pants. He pulled her body across the conference table, pulled her dress above her waist, and adjusted himself, ready to penetrate her. It was more than the excitement of the moment; it was her curvy frame, her luscious breasts, and the wet mound between her legs. He was captivated. Outside the door, the two security officers had stepped away for a second and walked down the hall.

"*J'ai entendu du bruit venant de la salle de conférence,*" said one of the guards.

"*Êtes-vous sûr? Je n'ai rien entendu,*" the other countered.

"*Allons voir,*" the taller of the two said as he peeked around the corner at the conference lounge.

"*J'ai pensé que cette porte était fermée,*" said the shorter guard.

"*Peut-être le vent,*" said the guard, feeling more secure as he tucked his Ruger into his pants and walked toward the balcony to close the French doors.

Out of nowhere, Dutch dropped from the sky, his foot held in place by the rope he had used to drop himself from the roof of the building.

"What the fuck?" the guard said, just as Dutch let off a round, shooting him in the chest at point-blank range as the other guard pulled his gun from his holster. Dutch shot him in the head, the silencer muffling the gunfire.

He opened the door to the conference room, where Tita was hammering away at Dutch's Charlie. He grabbed Tita around his neck, his penis still penetrating Clair, her legs in midair as she watched Tita's eyes pop out of his startled head.

"Wha..." He could speak no more as Dutch tightened his grip.

"This isn't personal, Mr. President," Dutch said, before he slit the man's throat like a pig's.

Blood squirted all over Clair's gown, but she didn't mind. She was just glad the escapade was over. As Dutch pulled Tita's body off her, his penis slid from between her legs as well.

"Thank God. What took you so long?"

"Hanging, baby, hanging in midair," he said, smiling as she got off the table and adjusted her gown, then her hair.

Clair watched as Dutch carefully let Tita's body slither to the floor beneath him. He then grabbed her arm and the two of them tiptoed back into the conference lounge and to the balcony where the cable and rope were waiting. He attached the cable and rope to a paling, then connected himself to Clair. They slid down the side of the building from the twentieth floor to the concrete sidewalk. Craze was conveniently waiting for them in a black bulletproof Hummer when they touched down.

Dutch and Clair walked hand in hand as if they were two lovers spending a night on the town. He opened the door to the bulletproof truck and waited for her to take the backseat. Then he too got into the truck and closed the door. Craze sped off down the street. Dutch reached into his pocket and pulled out a cell phone, dialing a number.

Odouwo answered and smiled his notorious smile as he hung up and put the phone back in his jacket pocket. Still in the ballroom, he walked over to the other Charlies.

"It's time we go. Let's move quickly," he said. They all calmly left the party one by one and got into the limousine waiting outside for them along with Odouwo's men. The hit had been successful.

An hour later, Tita's two other officers returned from their dinner break. It was then that they discovered the two dead security guards lying on the balcony of the conference lounge. One of the men opened the door to the conference room and called for the president but there was no response. The guard drew his gun, as did the other guard, as they went inside, where they found Tita in a pool of blood.

The uniformed officer bent over Tita's body, his fingers feeling for the carotid artery to take Tita's pulse, but there was none.

"*Le président est mort,*" said the shaken security officer kneeling over Tita's corpse. "*Oh, mon Dieu, le président a été assassiné. Appel quelqu'un pour le secourir, vite!*"

KISS OF DEATH

Two Weeks Later
Abuja, Nigeria

It was close to midnight and thousands of voters had gathered in a large field awaiting the results of what media outlets around the world were calling a "forced" presidential election. The country had been in a state of disorder ever since Tita's assassination, which had resulted in a state of emergency. But, even though the media had managed to poison the minds of viewers, the people of Nigeria were relieved and ready for a new leader now that Tita was out of office. They wanted someone to take over who cared about them and would provide the necessities, such as fresh water, shelter, medical treatment, and schooling for the young.

Mr. Odouwo, Dutch, and Craze were sitting in a restaurant at the bar waiting for the votes to be tallied. The bar was packed; there was not an inch of space. It was like Times Square on New Year's Eve. And when the polls came in indicating that

Yusef Odouwo had won by a landslide, the huge crowd cheered with such total excitement that even Dutch was forced to jump for joy. Yusef arrived minutes later in a limousine and the people cheered even louder. He stood at the podium to deliver his victory speech.

"My people of Nigeria, we have been victorious! This is a very big moment! Not just for me but mainly for you! It is you who need change! It is you who need liberation! It is you who need to take care of your families! Too many of us die, not being able to live a decent and good life! And it's not because we don't want to, but it's because we have been denied for far too long! This is an opportunity to fulfill who we are! And as your president, I want you to succeed! I want Nigeria and its people to not suffer anymore. We have suffered for far too long! I tell you, my people, the suffering ends tonight!"

The crowd cheered as Yusef waited patiently for them to calm down.

"My people of Nigeria, I plan to build up our beautiful nation as it once was and bring salvation to Nigeria! I was born to be your leader, and I won't let you down! I promise you we are going to build together. I promise you, everyone will get more freedom and choices as long as I am president!"

The crowd began to chant "Odouwo for president." Yusef smiled at how everything was taking shape.

"I'd like for my nephew to please take the stage," he said, looking to his left through the massive crowd of people until his eyes found his nephew's.

Mr. Odouwo quickly left Dutch and Craze and made his way through the mass of people and stood on the stage next to his uncle. He looked out into the crowd as they cheered and chanted the Odouwo name. It was then that Dutch realized

Mr. Odouwo's plan. He could now see it. The takeover was evident. With Tita out the way, Yusef Odouwo would control the country. Dutch realized all he had done in the streets of Newark was small and minute compared to what he had helped do for Nigeria; knowing now that his murderous ways had just gone global and international put a smile on his face.

Over the next few months Mr. Odouwo and Dutch obtained thirty-seven diamond mines scattered throughout the continent of Africa. Some mines were more plentiful than others, but overall, Mr. Odouwo kept his part of the deal and made Dutch a partner in the diamond trade. Mr. Odouwo had access to the richest, most powerful and elite socialites in the world. He would sell the diamonds to Europe's prized privileged, then send his henchmen to steal back the precious stones. After a fatal robbery left one of his henchmen dead on the scene, Dutch decided that it would be he and Craze who would steal the diamonds back instead of Mr. Odouwo's unreliable security team.

"I don't know," said Mr. Odouwo when Dutch confronted him and told him how the deals would be carried out in the future. "What do you know about stealing?"

Dutch smiled his infamous grin. Stealing was how he got his start in life. He thought back to the good old days when he used to steal cars down at the port.

Mr. Odouwo technically had no choice or options when dealing with Dutch. He unfortunately was in the same boat with everyone else, and what Dutch wanted Dutch always got.

So Mr. Odouwo would sell the diamonds, then Dutch and Craze would steal them back. Then Mr. Odouwo would auction the diamonds off to the highest bidder only to have them stolen yet again. This was big business for him. But the even bigger business was the rarest of stones, which he was collecting for himself. Of course no one knew about his little secret of skimming off the top, nor did anyone know how much he valued the meticulous jewels. But one day soon, someone would dare to find out.

Dutch and Craze collaborated in the most brilliant of the schemes to steal back Odouwo's diamonds after he sold them. It was second nature to them, easy pickings. Dutch and Craze were cold, heartless assassins and wouldn't hesitate to kill anyone standing in their way. Both successfully accomplished many a coup together for Odouwo, but it was the first one, the weirdest of all, that Dutch would never forget. How could he—Madrid, Spain, in springtime. His mission: to steal a set of clear yellow diamonds from the royal family, who were the descendants of King Ferdinand. King Ferdinand was the royal heir who funded Christopher Columbus's search for a western route to Asia. Dutch arrived at the Casa de Villa, owned by Fernando Enrique. Fernando was a middle-aged man who lived off his family's two-century-old wine empire. Fernando spent his wealth frivolously on expensive yachts, buying private islands, and purchasing dinosaur fossils, but his greatest fetish was diamonds.

Fernando would scour the world looking for the rarest of diamonds to enhance his already consummate collection. Dutch was aware that Fernando would be away on business the night he was to break into his villa. The estate was heavily guarded, but that wouldn't stop Dutch from getting inside. He attached a silencer to his nine and pulled a mask over his face. He wanted to make the heist clean, with as little complication as possible. The back of any perimeter was always just as protected as the front, if not more so. But Dutch knew better than to walk straight through the front door. Two armed guards stood at the entrance gate talking in their native tongue. Talking made the time go by faster and brought them laughter and excitement. Unfortunately for them, tonight was the wrong night for them to be looking for excitement, because it had already showed up in its worst form: Dutch.

"Oye, tú viste eso?" asked one of the guards, pointing to some bushes near the side gate. He could have sworn he had seen something moving.

"No, yo no vi nada," responded the other guard, figuring his partner could handle it. *"Vengo ahora, tengo que usar el baño,"* he added, thinking it was nothing, before he walked away from his post to take a leak.

The other guard loosened his gun in its holster, his hand gently resting on the barrel, just in case he needed quick access to his pistol. He walked closer to the bushes, making sure the coast was clear. He never noticed Dutch lying flat on the ground with his gun pointed upward, silently waiting for the guard to fall into his trap. His eyes were somewhere else until he was right on top of Dutch. And then it was too late. The guard quickly pulled his weapon out of the holster, but never had a chance to aim. Dutch had already fired the first shot as soon as the guard looked his way. The bullet pierced his forehead, blowing out the back of the guard's skull. He was dead before his body hit the ground. Quickly, Dutch stripped him of his uniform so he could give himself the advantage. Now, he looked just like one of them.

"Adónde tú estabas que duraste tanto?" asked the guard, zippering up his pants, as he realized who he thought was his partner wasn't. He quickly tried to reach for his gun, but Dutch was too quick.

"English, motherfucker, English," Dutch said, raising his pistol without warning and letting off twice in the guard's face as he walked by him.

There were other guards on the sides of the house, a few more located in the rear. It didn't matter, though, as the guards had been ordered not to leave their posts and never did unless told to. Dutch quickly hid the bodies of the two dead security guards in the bushes.

Dutch now had his way in and his way out. He walked up to the front door and shot out the lock, causing the Spanish pueblo doors to stand ajar. Just as he had wanted to, Dutch walked right through the front doors. A huge Swarovski crystal chandelier hung in the foyer, as did the beginning of an assortment of rare and expensive paintings from all over the world, by artists such as Jackson Pollock and Willem de Kooning. There was a double spiral staircase. Dutch had been told to take the left side to the upstairs floor and find the third door on the left of the hall, which was Fernando's office. It was there that Fernando kept the jewels locked safely away. Dutch ran up the staircase and walked down the hall looking for Fernando's office. He opened the third door on the left, and sure enough it was the office. Dutch hurried inside, closing the door behind him. He knew he didn't have much time. He had to find the jewels and escape undetected, if possible.

Dutch began looking around. The drawers of a mahogany desk were locked, causing Dutch to believe that what he was looking for was in one of them. He took out his military-style knife and popped the lock on the top drawer. He looked through the drawer only to find dictation tapes, Post-its and other office supplies.

"Can I help you find something?"

Dutch heard the woman's voice as he was popping the lock on another drawer. He looked up at her as he reached for his gun. She had to be the most beautiful woman Dutch had ever seen in his life. He wondered what man would dare to touch her. She wore a long black silk night slip that hugged every curve on her perfectly voluptuous body. She had golden skin with long, flowing black hair and piercing grayish-blue eyes.

Dutch had been all over the world and had slept with women who would make Tiger Woods jealous, but he had never run across such a striking figure until now.

What is she doing? He knew he had to be extra careful. Heedlessness might cost him his life.

"You don't need your gun. I'm only here to help you," she said, in her Colombian accent, looking like an exact replica of Penelope Cruz.

"It would be foolish of me to believe you, don't you think?" Dutch asked as he pointed his gun at her.

"It would be foolish of you to rummage through desk drawers looking for something that's not there when there are other security guards roaming the property, don't you think?" she asked sarcastically, sipping a glass of Domaine Ott as they both looked out the window at one of the security guards standing at his post.

"How do you know I'm looking for something?" he asked her, intrigued and puzzled at the same time.

"Why else would you be here...um...let's see, money or maybe..." she smiled, leaning toward him, then she whispered, "maybe...diamonds."

Dutch gave her a puzzled look. "You want to play games and I got shit to do, lady," he said, no longer seeing her as a threat, but still not understanding her position.

She smiled at him before she spoke.

"And I figured that and I'm here to help you. I did say that before, didn't I? Why are you still pointing that gun at me?"

"Stop!"

"What?" she asked, freezing in her tracks and looking around the room, as if something big was about to happen.

"Oh, never mind," Dutch said, tired of her beauty, tired of her questions, and tired of playing her games in the middle of his jewelry heist. He lowered his gun.

"*Gracias.*"

She slowly opened the office door, making sure the coast was clear.

"*Ven.*" She turned to him, using her hand to signal him to follow her, and he did. In the back of his mind, he kept telling himself he was absolutely crazy. He didn't know what to think. But something told him he wouldn't find out just by standing there.

She took Dutch by the hand, then walked into an open room, the master bedroom suite.

She walked over to a painting hanging on the wall.

"Do you like this painting?"

"I do, it's a great piece," Dutch said as they both stared at the painting hanging on the wall.

"It is a Picasso, an original, worth over twenty million dollars. For the past year my husband could not even sleep until he had his hands on this painting. Let me ask you a question. Do you think this painting is worth more than a human life?" the woman asked.

"It all depends."

"Depends on what?"

"Whose life we're talking about."

"Would that painting be worth more to you than me?" she asked him, tears in her eyes, as if he was some mirror, mirror, on the wall who would say what she wanted to hear.

"Not if I loved you," he said calmly, hoping that was the answer she already knew.

Dutch tucked his gun in waistband and lifted the picture. Behind it an eighteen-by-eighteen safe was implanted neatly in the wall. Dutch raised his eyebrows and looked at the woman.

"I told you I was trying to help you," she said, shrugging her shoulders.

"Why?"

She put down her glass and worked on the combination to the safe.

Dutch was so confused by the woman's disposition that he had to question it. "Who are you?"

"I'm Veles Enrique, Fernando's wife," she chuckled at him.

"If you're his wife, why are you helping me?"

"Because..." she said, deciding not to confide in him. "You wouldn't understand," she snapped as she began to twirl the knob, entering the combination.

"Still, you are his wife, and yet you help me steal hi—"

Before Dutch could say another word, she spun around, facing him, her face telling the story of a woman devastatingly scorned.

"My husband doesn't love me...he loves someone else...he is with her as we speak."

She fell silent as a tear rolled down her face. She moved away, composed herself, and turned to him. "All this..." she said, holding her arms up, referring to the twenty-thousand-square-foot mansion filled with priceless statues, art, jewels, and furnishings passed down from Fernando's royal heirs. "This is the most empty place you could imagine being in, and I am a painting on the wall."

Dutch understood her now. Fernando didn't love his wife, he simply had the "perfect" wife to complete the picture of "perfect."

"That is my life, and I must say that a life without love is no life at all," she said as one tear dropped. She turned and finished entering the combination.

"What you want is in that box," she said, as if he need not touch anything else.

Dutch reached inside the safe and pulled out the box, believing her. He sat on the bed to evaluate its contents. As he lifted the lid, multiple flares of colorful light escaped from the box. He was captivated as he looked at all the priceless gems. Not only did he now have the clear and canary diamonds he had come there for, he had Fernando's entire collection. Dutch closed the box and stood.

"It's time to go now," he said, holding in his palm what he had come for.

"Yes, I'd say it is, now that you've got what you came for," she said, not realizing he could read her mind.

Dutch heard the sarcasm, but simply ignored her, moving close to her so that he was on top of her as he stood toe to toe with her. So close, he could smell musk and vanilla scents from her perfume. Unable to resist her, he took her in his arms, holding her tightly as he kissed her lips, igniting a wildfire between two souls.

"Maybe you're what I came for," he suggested, pulling back from her embrace and looking into her eyes to see where her head was at.

"If I were, you wouldn't be holding my husband's diamonds,

would you now?" she asked, jealous that he was there for the stones.

"This is circumstance; these aren't for me," he said, being perfectly clear that she could easily become a kidnap victim. Making that shit happen right now was going through his mind, too. He couldn't stop looking at her; she was so beautiful he wanted to kiss her on the mouth again, and kissing women was a "never", for him.

"Thank you," she said, wishing she was being kidnapped, and sexually seduced as well.

Dutch knew it was time to roll out. He had what he came for, what the hell was he still standing there for? *Look, I'm stuck right here. I swear she's so beautiful I can't stop looking at her. She's a fucking painting that you can't stop looking at.* Her beauty had captivated him. He bent to her ear, whispered to her a special secret, and then walked down the hall to the staircase. Once he reached the bottom, he turned. She was standing at the top of the staircase, her eyes pleading for him not to go. He turned and walked out the front double doors he had come in. Still wearing the uniform, he returned a nod at one of the guards who was watching him as he walked toward the gate. Dutch could see Craze sitting in a black Mercedes waiting for him. As soon as Craze started the car, Dutch turned to the guard and waved good-bye, hopping into the passenger seat. Then Craze sped them away.

The next morning, Fernando came home from spending the night with his mistress to find that the guards stationed at the front gate had abandoned their post. *What the hell am I paying these people for? Where are they?* he wondered, not thinking there was anything wrong. He let himself through the gate and proceeded up a flight of stairs carrying a Louis Vuitton bag in his hand. As he walked into the master suite he dropped his bags and stared around the room, realizing his prize possessions were no longer there. His wife was sprawled across their bed, her body lying still next to an empty bottle of sleeping pills. He looked over at the wall. His Picasso painting was lying on the floor and his safe was opened. He ran over to it. His heart sank as he looked inside. His box of priceless gems was gone. He actually began to cry as he realized he had been robbed of the precious jewels. He sank into a chair near the king-sized bed and looked at Veles, her body still warm.

"Even in death, you are still beautiful," he whispered to her.

He lifted himself and walked out of the room, closing the bedroom door behind him. He went into his office and began to play video footage of the night before. He watched his own wife leading the intruder into their bedroom. *How dare she betray me?* he thought to himself as he picked up the phone and called for the authorities. He continued watching the tape as he hung up the phone and slowly sat in his alligator-skin high-back chair. He opened a twenty-four-karat gold-plated humidor and picked Gurkha's, His Majesty's Reserve, the most expensive cigar in the world, infused with Louis XIII Cognac. He held the cigar under his nose, inhaling deeply the flavorful aroma. He cut off the television monitor, sat down, lit the cigar, and exhaled.

GREEN-EYED BANDIT

Newark, New Jersey

We just found his body." Those were the words that had awakened Nina out of her sleep every night ever since she heard the news reporter claim they had found Dutch's body.

It had been over three months now, but it seemed like yesterday when she hustled down to the courthouse, ready to confess her undying love for a man she barely knew yet couldn't let go of. She remembered the courthouse massacre as if it were yesterday. She had finally made up her mind to commit to him. She knew exactly what that commitment would involve, as Dutch was on trial for the Month of Murder and was looking at life in prison. So there would be prison visits, absent holidays, appeal denials, disappointments, the dream and the nightmare of it all. But it was okay, she was ready...until she heard the reporter on the radio.

"Yes, this is Miriam Roughneen reporting for Channel 11

News from the Essex County Courthouse, where today's trial ended in a deadly bloodbath."

In a daze, she heard the reporter but couldn't believe what was being said. Tears welled in her eyes. It hit her. It was over. She listened as the reporter ran off names of the dead, and she prayed his would not be included. A horn honked behind her and she pulled her car over to the side of the road. She couldn't drive, her emotions wouldn't let her, and as she realized the reality of the situation tears began to stream down her face.

The reporter finished the list of names. Nina had prayed that she wouldn't say Dutch's, and she hadn't. Relief filled her and she thanked God, knowing that they were destined to be together. She put the car in drive and continued heading for the courthouse. But by the time Nina got there, the police had blocked off the area. Luckily, she found parking and it was then that she heard the reporter speaking with Detective Smalls.

"We just found his body." Those were the words still ringing through her. She dropped her small purse on the passenger seat as her body went limp.

Nina jumped out of her sleep as the morning sun rose, realizing she was having another nightmare, the words still ringing through her head. "We found his body."

She made her way into her bathroom and washed her face in the sink, realizing her hands were trembling. She looked at them, rubbing them to get them to stop. She rinsed them under cold water, splashing her face once more before turning off the faucet. *I miss you so much*, she thought as a sea of tears streamed down her face. Nina had never gotten the chance to tell Dutch just how much she truly loved him. By the time she reached the courthouse it was too late. The police had the entire place taped off.

Nina dressed in a rush, not wanting to be late for work. She was assistant branch manager and was responsible for opening the bank, which meant it was her job to be the first one there.

She threw her jacket over her shoulders, closed her front door behind her, and hopped into her car. She had a briefcase and a cup of coffee, which she managed to juggle carefully as she sat the coffee in the holder and her briefcase on the passenger seat. She started the car, threw it into drive, and headed down the street. Maybe it was her imagination, but she always had the same daydream that Dutch would be waiting for her inside the bank when she opened the door. Only he would be so clever as to be seated at her desk.

Occupied in the daydream of finding Dutch in the bank, Nina didn't even see a car speeding through the intersection she was crossing. Out of nowhere, the vehicle slammed into the tail end of the passenger side of her car. She spun around in the intersection, turning a complete 360 degrees. Shaken, but all right, she looked out the window at the other driver in the car that had just crashed into her, damaging the entire side panel, lights, and bumper of her car.

A few days later she went to an auto body shop. The insurance, of course, would cover the damages. She just had to get her car fixed. She pulled up in front of the auto body shop and got out to see if someone could help her. Before she could take another step, one of the mechanics was already in front of her.

"I'm Dwight Gaines. How can I help you, ma'am?" Dwight asked as he wiped the oil off his hands with a rag.

"Um...I had an accident. Someone ran into the side of my car," Nina said, pointing out the obvious.

Dwight walked around the side of the car as Nina walked behind him.

"Looks like four, maybe five hundred dollars," said Dwight, looking to see if that was acceptable for her.

"Really?" Nina was surprised.

"Yeah, all I got to do is pound out your fender, buff it up a bit, then paint it. I can get that done right away for you, two, maybe three days tops."

Nina dropped the car off and two days later Dwight called from the auto body shop. When Nina got there, her car looked as good as new.

"Wow, that's a great job. You really know your stuff," said Nina, smiling at the tall, brown-skinned mechanic.

"Yup, it's what I do," said Dwight, stroking the side of his face.

"Well, I'm impressed," she said, following him over to the counter.

"Here's the bill," he said, presenting her with the slip.

Nina looked at the balance, it was $422.83. She took out her checkbook and wrote a check to Dwight's Auto Body.

"Wow, I don't know how to thank you," she said, all smiles as he handed her the keys to her car.

"How about letting me take you to dinner?" he asked, hoping she would say yes.

"Sure, why not. Dinner it is," she said, exchanging numbers with him over the counter.

Four days later, they went out on their first date, and then again, every night thereafter.

Copenhagen, Denmark

Eight months after taking Fernando Enrique for his precious jewels, which turned out to be worth more than the Picasso painting hiding them in the wall, Dutch found himself in the capital of Denmark. He was there in pursuit of a twelve-carat green diamond, which he was to acquire at an auction, of all places. Dutch wasn't there to bid, he was there to steal it from the buyer. His intended target was Paavo Bixby. He was the richest man in Denmark, with a transportation empire that supported the entire railway and airline systems for all of Scandinavia.

Bixby requested that the auction be held at the Nationalmuseet, Denmark's largest museum of cultural history. He wanted to host the auction at an immense venue so as many people as possible could witness him outbid all the wealthy attendees.

Dutch got seated in the last row and was handed an auction paddle right before the bidding began. The first item to be auctioned off was a champagne saltwater pearl necklace that had been worn by the queen of France. After five minutes of bidding the necklace was sold to a Polish businessman for six hundred thousand. Bixby was seated in the first row, and Dutch had a clear view of him. He noticed that after ten bids Bixby had not raised his paddle once. Dutch knew he was waiting to put all his money on the green stone, which would be the last bid of the evening.

When the green diamond was finally brought to the auction block, the bidding began at $250,000. A gentleman in the right-hand corner of the room challenged Bixby until the bid for the diamond was $950,000.

"Nine hundred and fifty thousand going once, going twice, and sold to the man here in the front row," the auctioneer said, pointing to Bixby. Dutch smiled and left the museum before Bixby claimed his item, then took pictures with his diamond for the local newspaper. He walked out of the museum along with a security guard where his driver was holding the door to his Rolls Royce Phantom. They traveled down the road, never noticing the Hummer following behind them. Bixby gaped at his diamond, unable to take his eyes off it, just as the Hummer slammed into the rear of the Phantom. The collision caused Bixby to drop the diamond to the floor of the car. He turned around to see the Hummer ramming into the rear of the Phantom again.

"Drive faster! Drive faster!" Bixby demanded.

He'd never been in a situation like this before. One minute everything was fine, the next, disaster. The driver stepped on the gas but Craze kept up with the car and was soon right beside them. Craze rammed the car on the side until it eventually veered off the road and into a ditch.

Bixby's door wouldn't open, trapping him in the car from his side. His driver rolled down the window and tried to emerge from the vehicle but was met with four bullets to the chest and died instantly. Bixby feared for his life as blood from his driver splattered all over the toffee-colored leather interior.

Dutch looked inside the car at Bixby shaking in his pants.

"Where's the diamond?" Dutch asked in a calm tone. Bixby looked up and saw the barrel of a Smith & Wesson .38 staring at him.

Bixby nervously pointed to the floor, hoping his life would be spared in exchange for the jewel. But he was wrong. Dutch looked down at the floor where Bixby was pointing and saw the green diamond he was there for. He pointed the gun at

Bixby and began to fire at point-blank range. Dutch grabbed the green diamond from the floor and jumped back into the Hummer as Craze drove off like nothing had happened. He drove them straight to the airport, where Mr. Odouwo had a private jet waiting to fly them back to France.

FED UP

Two Years Later
Los Angeles

Kimberly Nicole Reese was far from the toughest girl coming up through school. She got into a lot of fights and lost most of them. The lack of respect she had received as a youth led her to a career in which respect would be given, not necessarily earned. She became a Philadelphia police officer. After a few years on the force Kim, as everyone called her, wanted to do something that would make her tougher than patrolling the streets of Philly ever could. She sought to become an FBI agent. She took the required knowledge test and went through training camp with flying colors. After graduation she was sent to the West Coast and reported to the Federal Bureau of Investigation's Los Angeles office.

Her first big case as a field agent was to assist Agent Vincent Shipp, a hard-nosed agent who was in his seventh year with the Bureau. Their assignment was to track down a Mexican drug lord, Chico Dego, who flooded narcotics throughout Long Beach, Compton, Watts, and other cities by way of Tijuana. They finally got a tip that Chico was lying low in a beach house in Santa Cruz. They set up surveillance in a carpet-cleaning van down the street and tapped the phone lines. They kept a watch of the home to see if Chico would make his presence known.

Kim was assigned to watch the house and report any movement or activity. She watched for two days straight, with no signs of Chico. All she saw was his men going in and out all day long. After a long day of looking through binoculars, Kim finally saw the man of the hour, Chico Dego himself. Chico walked out on the back deck of the house and lit a cigarette. Kim identified him by distinctive tattoos he had on both his arms. The diced-up crucifix on his right arm and upside-down angel with her legs wide open exposing her private area on his left were listed in his profile.

Chico wasn't a very tall guy, or even muscular, for that matter, but his treacherous ways stood out to everyone who had ever heard of him. He once killed a priest in Acapulco for not letting a drug transaction take place in front of him. His gang had been under watch for the past year, and this was actually the first time he had allowed himself to go outside. This casual smoke break would cost him dearly.

Kim and Agent Shipp watched as Chico flicked his cigarette onto the sandy beach.

"I hope that smoke was worth it, my friend, because we are coming for you," Agent Shipp said, lowering his binoculars as Chico went back through the sliding door.

"So when do we go in?" Kim asked, a little nervous. Agent Shipp could read her like an open book and knew she was scared as hell.

"Relax, rookie. We're not going to go after 'em until nightfall. That is as long as he stays put. But if that son of a bitch takes one foot toward the front door we're going to slam his ass like a grizzly bear on steroids. He won't get away," Agent Shipp said, his words a far cry from comforting for Kimberly. She just wasn't sure if she was ready or if she could handle the pressure under fire.

It was 9:22 P.M. and Chico had not made any attempt to leave the house. Agent Shipp had all his field agents in place around the property, ready to strike. Kim followed Agent Shipp as he crept along the beach, up against a sea cliff. They climbed up the grassy hill, an army of agents close behind. Kim's brow was now dripping with sweat and her palms were clammy. *This is it*, she thought to herself. In a few moments she would have to invade the house and do what the FBI had been trying to accomplish for the last year: capture Chico Dego, one of the most lethal drug lords to come out of Mexico in recent years. Agent Shipp gave her the nod and she got on the walkie-talkie and gave the field agents the go-ahead. They were now ready to turn Chico Dego's world upside-down. Kimberly made sure her vest was on tight.

Chico Dego sat on the couch with his bare feet up on the center glass table, drinking a Corona and watching the Spanish network, Telemundo. He had a few chicas running around the house with his hands chasing behind them. Chico could have women any time he wanted, but at the moment, he preferred to just kick back and watch a couple of shows and drink some cold ones. He had no idea the FBI were right outside his door, but he was about to find out. Before Chico could remove the Corona bottle from his lips, the front door flew open, and in poured field agents, moving in unison, holding high-powered assault weapons.

"FBI! Get on the floor, now!" one of the field agents shouted as they rushed forward.

Chico decided he wasn't going out with his tail between his legs. He dropped down and pulled an M-16 from under the seat cushions and fired away. He then jumped behind the couch, preparing to avoid the hail of bullets that was going to come his way. The field agents took cover as well, shooting up the glass tables and lamps in the process. Chico's two men heard the shots and ran from the back room with guns in hand ready to take on their adversaries.

Agent Shipp and Kimberly were behind the wall that led into the living room where the gunfire was coming from. Agent Shipp spotted Chico as he was slipping through the gunfire and down the hall into one of the back rooms.

"Hey, rookie, we can't let Chico get away. Go around the back of the building, in case he tries to get away out the back," said Agent Shipp, thinking of the river not too far away. Kimberly went back downstairs and ran to the side of the house, careful to look up at the windows. She knew he could come out a window in an attempt to escape. But she held her pistol, fearless and ready, hoping she didn't have to use it, not today.

The Mexicans managed to kill a field agent and injure two others, relieving some of the force that was going against them. They didn't see Agent Shipp approaching from behind, and by the time one of the Mexicans realized Agent Shipp was there, his partner was already dead. The lone Mexican aimed his gun at his new target but Agent Shipp was too fast for him. Agent Shipp laid him down with a single shot, shattering his skull. The field agents ceased fire while the two men were down. All they could hear was the women screaming in the background.

Agent Shipp cautiously approached the hallway, stepping

over the bodies of the Mexicans. He had the other field agents following closely behind him, securing the area and making sure there were no more surprises. Agent Shipp tried turning the knob to fling back the door but it was locked. He gave his agents a look and signaled for them to stand back, then shot through the doorknob. As the door flung open, Chico began firing a barrage of gunfire.

"It's over, Chico! Your men are dead! There's nowhere left for you to go. Come on, don't let this day end like this, my friend. Come on, be smart! Let the girls go and give yourself up!" Agent Shipp said, trying to talk him down once Chico's gunfire ceased while he changed the clip in his weapon.

"Fuck you, pig! I'm not going back to no fucking prison, motherfucker! We end it today, we end it now," Chico said before letting off another shot.

Agent Shipp knew that Chico wouldn't surrender and would probably fight to his death. Agent Shipp was prepared for that outcome. He was ready to put an end to the standoff.

"Okay, men. This asshole is just as good to us dead as he is alive, so if he wants to press his own stop button so be it, but we end this now.

In the middle of Agent Shipp's message they heard a single shot come from the room, followed by screams and a loud thud. Agent Shipp assumed Chico had taken himself out, but he was wrong.

"I just killed one of the girls, assholes! Back off before I do another one! *Comprende?*"

Agent Shipp didn't want any more innocent women getting killed but knew backing down wasn't an option either. For all he knew, Chico was going to kill the girls anyway. He decided to proceed as planned and try to save them in the process.

Chico stood his ground, waiting for the agents to move back. He had his gun pointed at the back of one of the remaining girls' head just in case the agents didn't cooperate. He was prepared to end her life just as easily as the girl before her. What he didn't realize was that Shipp never played by the rule book. So, he wouldn't be backing down. Shipp made the next move, a gutsy one, but one still within his character. He rolled in front of the door with his gun extended, hoping to have Chico's head in his sight, but he didn't. Chico was hiding behind two girls, so no one could get a good shot at him.

"It's over, Chico! Move away from the girls now!" Agent Shipp commanded. Chico didn't say anything and kept his gun held at the girl's head. He was showing the agents that he would still kill the girls. "Either you move away from the girls or we'll shoot through them just to get to you! You make the call!" Agent Shipp said, giving him an ultimatum.

Chico finally realized he was running out of options. The agents weren't backing down and he would be dead within thirty seconds if he didn't surrender. Since he didn't want to go to prison just yet, he decided on the next best thing, he ran . . .

Chico pushed the two girls into Agent Shipp's path to could create a diversion and shot out the bedroom window as he ran toward it. Agent Shipp moved the girls out of his way, then ran into the room, trying to get a shot at Chico. As Chico dived out the window, bullets from Agent Shipp's gun missed him, hitting the window frame.

Kimberly looked up at the sound of shattered glass as an airborne Chico noticed her immediately and began to rain bullets on her, hoping to kill her before he hit the ground. Kimberly fired at her target. The bullets missed Chico, but he hit Kimberly once in the chest, causing her to fall to the ground. As she went down, he thought he was safe and had a clear chance to get away, but before his feet touched the ground the back of his head exploded as Agent Shipp was looking down on Chico's dead body still holding his smoking gun through the window.

"I got 'em," he said looking back at the other agents. The girls were still screaming and crying, but were glad it was all over.

Kimberly was sitting up looking at Chico's body when Agent Shipp and the other field agents came running out the side door to her aid.

"Are you all right, rookie?" Agent Shipp asked.

"Yeah, my vest saved me," she said as Agent Shipp looked at the bullet caught in the vest.

"I want this vest. Let's run this bullet through forensics along with his gun," said Agent Shipp.

Then he added, "What happened, Agent Reese? You had a clear shot at him."

"I, um...hesitated, I guess," said Kimberly, rubbing her throbbing chest area.

"Well, when you finally learn how to shoot, maybe you'll never know how a bullet really feels. All that simulated bullshit they teach you in the academy won't work out here. You got to be naturally born to do this shit," Agent Shipp said, criticizing her.

"The next time I get shot at I'll keep that in mind just for you, sir," Kimberly said scornfully.

"I just saved your life, rookie, and you're standing here giving me shit? Let's see how long you make it out there."

Agent Shipp walked off, giving Kimberly some time to think about what he had said. Even though he was right, she didn't care to hear his opinion. She appreciated the fact that he had saved her life, but she could survive on her own. After that day she didn't speak to Shipp again. And deep inside she vowed to prove him wrong.

Following four years of hard, career-advancing work, Kimberly was called in by her superior for a brief meeting. This was the meeting that would change her life forever.

"Agent Reese, please have a seat," the director said from behind his desk.

Kimberly closed the door and took a seat in front of him.

"Agent Reese, I just want to start off by saying you're doing a hell of a job, and I'm glad you're one of us."

"Why thank you, sir," Kimberly said in a monotone.

"Agent Reese, this case here in my hand is marked extremely classified. It's a top secret, undercover mission. Do you think you're up to the challenge?"

"Yes, of course, Director Burns."

Kimberly was excited. This would be her first chance to go deep undercover. She had been waiting for the chance to prove herself for the past four years. Plus, if this case was as Director Burns was indicating, it would help propel her through the ranks.

"This operation is top secret. The Bureau is after an escaped murderer named Bernard James and his treacherous gang of bandits. Have you ever heard of him?" The director opened up the file so Kimberly could see all of the mug shots.

"No, sir. I don't think that I have."

"James is a drug dealer out of Newark, New Jersey, who was looking at a life sentence but decided to shoot up the Essex County Courthouse, and unknown to the world, he escaped."

"I think I remember that story in the news. I thought James was reported dead, sir."

"Yes, it was merely reported so. It's been confirmed that James escaped and is at large. No one wants to blow the whistle and confess that a mistake was made, so we need to apprehend him first."

"Do we have any leads?" Kimberly questioned.

"She is it, right here," said Director Burns, pointing to Angel's picture as he held it up for Kimberly to get a good look. "She is currently at a federal women's prison in Alderson, West Virginia. The assignment is to go to prison and get close to Angel Alvarez, until she leads you to Dutch. Trust me, if he's alive, this woman right here will lead us to him. But, Reese, I have to tell you something...Angel Alvarez is a dangerous woman. She is also a lesbian, and the Bureau wants you to convince her that she can trust you."

"How will I do that?"

"Any way you can," said the director. "But trust me, it won't be easy. Alvarez is a tough cookie. She trusts no one, except her other gang members, called the Charlies, who from what we understand go 'both' ways," the director said, clearing his throat. "Listen, there's a lot on the line here. This guy killed a lot of innocent people; he's marked extremely dangerous. And Angel is his sidekick psychopath. Angel Alvarez is just as deadly as he is. I want you to take your time with this. Are you sure you're up to this?"

Kimberly thought about the assignment, running the pros and the cons through her mind. The fact that Angel was a lesbian didn't bother her. The Bureau was already aware of the fact that Reese had her share of experiences with women, even though she was currently in a heterosexual relationship. What did bother her was the thought of prison. That was the most unappealing part of the assignment. She didn't know if she could do jail for so long. The concept was locking up people, not being locked up.

"It appears that this may be a little too much for you, so how about I just get someone else to take the case?"

The director closed the folder, highly disappointed in Kimberly's reaction. Kimberly thought about her career and decided she couldn't make the biggest mistake of her life.

"Wait, Director. I want the assignment. I can handle it. I will get close to Alvarez and bring Bernard James in myself. Really, I can do it," Kimberly said intensely, showing the director a side of her he'd never seen.

"Okay, Reese. I'll give you a shot, but if the terrain gets too rough I'm pulling you out. You understand?"

"You won't have to do that, sir. I will get Bernard James if it's the last thing I do."

He began to tell her everything they knew about Angel Alvarez.

One-eyed Roc stood in his prison cell at his sink, brushing his full beard in the mirror. With the Muslim hair oil he used on it, it glistened almost as brightly as his freshly shaven head. Roc stepped back and admired himself. He thought he looked damn good. Some guys let prison get the best of them, stress them, age them. But not Roc. He took the time and brushed it off his shoulders like it was nothing. He looked better inside than he had when he was walking the streets. Prison must have slowed his aging process, because he could easily pass for twenty-five years old.

Roc mostly felt his vigorous appearance and calmness were due to his strong Islamic beliefs. He was no longer a callous menace but still acknowledged he needed self-improvement in order to get closer to Allah. The first step he made to re-create himself was to change his name from Roc to Rahman, meaning merciful, which coincided with his new beliefs. Over the years Rahman had grown to believe his zeal for Islam had helped him change completely, and now he was ready to work on getting back to his family, despite his life sentence.

"*As-Salaamu Alaikum, Ahki,*" Akbar said standing in the doorway of Rahman's cell.

"*Alaikum As-Salaam,*" Rahman replied, returning the greeting.

Akbar was Rahman's mentor, who was also from Newark and had a similar background. Akbur walked into Rahman's cell and held out a magazine.

"What's that?" Rahman inquired, looking at the rolled-up magazine.

Akbar showed him the cover. It was a copy of the new *Don Diva* magazine with a picture of Dutch, Qwan, Craze, Angel, Zoom, and Rahman himself on the cover. It was a photograph from way back in the day that he remembered well but showed no interest in looking at it.

"Come on, Ock, you know I don't keep up wit' that anymore," he told Akbar as he prepared for prayer.

Akbar heard what he said, but didn't pay him any mind. He left the *Don Diva* magazine in his cell anyway. And just as Akbar figured, curiosity got the best of him, and Rahman found himself flipping through pages until he came to the article on Angel. When he finished reading the article he couldn't believe Angel had won her appeal. Now that she was being released, he felt a sense of confidence that he stood a chance of winning his as well.

He could tell that Angel was still the same Angel. She hadn't allowed prison to change or reform her, not one single bit. But he had changed, and it made him wonder where that would now leave the two of them. To him, she was the enemy. Everything he stood for, she stood against. He grabbed his prayer rug and kufi, then headed for Jum'ah.

FLIP SIDE

Kimberly left the Bureau after her meeting with Director Burns. She knew exactly what he was asking. Her assignment involved more than just the average duty. It involved going undercover, which was always dangerous, but to get close to her target, Kimberly knew she would have to "get close," a little closer than close, to say the least. She thought of Jan, her lover for many years. They had broken up because Terrence was in the picture. She remembered the last time she had seen Jan as if it were yesterday.

"Why you got me waiting on you all the time and you never show up, or by the time you do it's so late the night is over? If you don't want to do this then just say so, I'll move on," Jan said, tired of Kimberly's bullshit.

"Jan, I'm so sorry, Terrence held me up. Please don't be mad."

"Fucking Terrence, I'm so tired of hearing about *Him*. I don't know what the fuck to do."

The relationship was rocky as it was. Kimberly was indecisive about her sexuality. What had started as experimental turned out to be habitual. And her relationship with Jan carried itself through college, the police academy, the FBI academy, and up to the present, and the entire time Jan was sucking her pussy, she was in a complete heterosexual relationship with Terrence. It was only months ago that Jan had finally told Kim she had to make a choice.

"I can't do this anymore. I can't stand the idea of you fucking him. How can you do that? I just can't. It's either him or me."

Jan had put the ultimatum out there for Kimberly to decide. The problem was holidays, birthdays, her family, her career, society, and everything else that confused her. A man equaled normalcy, and a man fit the picture of the perfect American dream. A man could give her children, her parents grandchildren, and all the things in between, and that was why Terrence had the upper hand, because Terrence had a real penis. She couldn't take Jan home for Christmas. Her mother would keel over and have a heart attack at the thought of her daughter's sexual perversions. No, Jan was meant to be a secret, Jan was her release, and Jan could have her, she just had to stay in her place. But Jan wanted more.

"Come on, Jan, you're asking me to choose between you and him. That's so unfair, don't you think?"

"No, no, I don't. Do you think it's fair to me that I'm left alone because you're with him? It's just like it was with Isabel. Don't you think I'm tired of going through this with you?" Jan asked, completely frustrated with her and her choices.

"Jan, please, it's not that. I just..."

"Just what?" asked Jan, already knowing the answer. "Go with him, just go with him," she said, slamming the door behind her in hopes that Kimberly would come running after her, begging her not to go, but she didn't.

Maybe I'm making a mistake, maybe I shouldn't stay with Terrence. Maybe I should be with Jan.

Kimberly drove home in silence, thinking of her future with Terrence. He didn't know she was gay. He'd never met Jan and she never spoke of Isabel, her first lesbian lover. She would never forget her, as long as she lived. It was a flyer she found near her car in a hotel parking lot. She bent down at the image of a beautiful naked woman with her legs spread open, fingering herself. The flyer read, "Have the Best Time of Your Life with the Most Beautiful Women in the World" and advertised Women Only Wednesdays. Every Wednesday that passed she remembered the flyer, wanting desperately to see. She dressed up, wearing a black ruffled hat and a silk scarf around her neck. She ended up sitting in the corner of the club the following Wednesday. She watched as a girl danced on top of the bar, squatting in front of a woman who gently caressed her ass, then spread her cheeks open and licked her, placing money in the girl's string. Kimberly couldn't help but to stare at the girls. Their bodies gyrating and simulating sexual desire interested her, and she felt desire warming between her legs the more she looked at them.

"Hey, honey, here you go," said a waitress wearing nothing but three stars. She had stars covering her nipple area and a G-string with a star covering the face of her pussy.

"Hey, Betty, get your fat ass over here, can't you see I'm thirsty, woman," asked Liv, holding up an empty glass. Liv was a regular who Betty served more than liquor to. Everybody in the strip club knew that Liv and Betty had been lovers for the past ten years.

"Wait a minute, can't you see I'm talking," she hollered back at her before turning to Kimberly, who was unable to stop staring at her breasts.

"I got something for that mouth of yours to do besides that," she said, thinking of how good Betty sucked her pussy.

"I'm sorry, I didn't order anything yet," Kimberly said to the waitress.

"Don't worry about it, honey. That girl right there at the bar bought it for you."

Kimberly looked at the waitress to see who she was talking about. Betty pointed over at the purchaser of the cocktail. She was pretty and smiled at Kimberly, then got up and began to walk over to the table.

"Thanks, Betty," said Isabel as she approached.

Isabel was a white girl, really aggressive, and positively one hundred percent in love with pussy. She loved sucking pussy, fucking pussy, and literally anything that involved women and their bodies. She was a bit older than Kimberly, being thirty-three. Kimberly wasn't even old enough to drink, and if it wasn't for the fact that she had a fake ID she wouldn't even be sitting there.

"May I join you?" The Italian woman flirtatiously asked as she watched Betty walk away.

"Sure, why not."

"Do you drink martinis?"

"Well, no, not really, but thank you," said Kimberly, raising the drink to her lips and sipping the alcohol, the strength of the liquor catching her off guard.

"Wow, that's strong," Kimberly said.

The woman smiled. "My name is Isabel. What's yours?"

"Kimberly."

"Well, it's nice to meet you, Kimberly," Isabel said, extending her hand.

"It's nice to meet you, too." Isabel didn't let go of Kimberly's hand. "You are very beautiful, Kimberly. How old are you?"

"I'm eighteen." Kimberly smiled innocently, feeling a little uncomfortable as Isabel moved her hand to Kimberly's lap and rubbed her leg. Her affection was strong and her pretty, soft face pulled Kimberly in.

"Would you like to dance?"

Kimberly didn't say anything. She looked at the dance floor and the other women dancing with each other.

"Come," said Isabel as she led her to the dance floor. As they danced to house music Kimberly felt very comfortable with Isabel. It was as if Isabel knew exactly what to say, exactly what to do, and exactly where to touch her. The more drinks Kimberly had the more open she became, the more seductive she felt, the more at ease she was with Isabel's constant touch and constant affection. Isabel was really feeling the energy between them and decided to kiss Kimberly, who willingly opened her mouth and kissed her back.

"Let's get out of here and go to my apartment," she said, kissing Kimberly on her earlobe.

"Okay," said Kimberly, knowing that Isabel was going to take her back to her apartment to have sex with her. Kimberly was a more than willing participant. She wanted to have sex with a woman, she wanted to suck on a woman's pussy, and she wanted a woman to suck on hers. She was completely in love with the female anatomy and had a secret desire to be with a woman that she could now fulfill.

One thing led to another and Kimberly let Isabel remove all of her clothes.

"I want to suck your pussy so bad, it's so wet," Isabel whispered as she slid her middle finger between Kimberly's legs, parting them, before sinking her tongue into Kimberly's wet pussy. Kimberly's body immediately began to climax, her pussy got so wet, tingly, and hot. Isabel knew exactly what to do to make her cum, and she made Kimberly do just that as she sucked her pussy, turning Kimberly inside out.

That was how it all began with Isabel, and for over a year, Isabel and Kimberly were lovers.

Kimberly drove in silence, thinking about her past lesbian lifestyle. *The Bureau must know. Why else would they ask me to go undercover, in prison, to get close to a psycho lesbian serial killer? Of course, they have to know.*

Kimberly thought about the assignment she had accepted and all that it would involve. She had looked at a picture of Angel in Director Burns's office. Kimberly was attracted to the Puerto Rican woman in the picture, imagining what she looked like with no clothes on and what she felt like. In the back of her mind, she heard Director Burns, and basically she knew exactly what he was asking of her. He was asking her to do whatever it took to get close to Angel Alvarez, even if that meant sleeping with her.

Kimberly pulled into the driveway of her apartment complex. Terrence was home, and she would have to break the news to him gently that she was going undercover and would be leaving for prison now that she had accepted the assignment.

Kimberly walked into her apartment a little after midnight and found that her fiancé, Terrence, was still up walking around. She found this unusual, since Terrence always went to bed every night no later than ten-thirty. He was a weatherman for ABC 7 News in San Francisco and had to be at work early. Kimberly went into the kitchen to see what he was up to.

"Hey, babe, I wasn't expecting you home this early," Terrence said as he closed the refrigerator door, glad she was there.

"I got an assignment today, undercover," Kimberly said, not really explaining the situation in detail.

"Yeah, you gonna have a lot of overtime?" he asked as he walked behind her, ready to mount her from behind. "Pull your skirt up, baby," he whispered in her ear, one hand fondling her breasts as the other traveled between her legs, under her panties, his fingers feeling her wet pussy.

She knew what time it was. It was no different in the morning. He'd wake up with a hard dick, go to the bathroom, and get back into bed, climbing on top of her.

"Kimberly, come on, spread your legs."

She could be lying there half asleep, but he didn't care—he needed his release when he needed it. She could claim a headache or say she was tired, it didn't matter, he didn't want to hear it. His response was simple: "Just bend over, Kimberly, and spread your legs."

"Honey, I had a hard day and I need to talk to you," said Kim as he pulled her skirt up around her waist, playing with her pussy.

"Just bend over, Kimberly, and spread your legs," he said, commanding her to do as he said.

He slid her panties down to her heels, bending her over the back of the sofa as he entered her from behind, pushing inside her and pulling himself out as he held her legs apart, banging out her back as if she was a blow-up doll.

"You been a good girl, huh? Whose pussy is this? You better not let nobody fuck this pussy but me, you understand?" he said, holding her neck as he fucked her harder and faster, taking less than five minutes to ejaculate inside her, his body sweating bullets. He humped her slowly, letting out every drop of cum he had, sticking his dick in her as far as it would go. She was trapped as his dick held her pussy spread apart until he was ready to slowly slide out of her and let her go.

She was still bent over the sofa, fully dressed, ass exposed. He walked away from her and down the hallway to the bathroom. Kimberly pulled her panties back up and smoothed her skirt down as if nothing had happened. The two would now resume as if sex had never happened.

"I have to tell you something," she called out, not sure how to break the news.

"One minute," he said before returning to the living room where she was waiting for him. "So what's going on, baby," he said as he sat on the couch, picked up the remote, and turned on the television.

Kimberly watched him, lifting the remote from his hand and pushing the little red button with her thumb.

"Hey, why you do that?" he said, his attention completely focused on her as she snatched the remote away from him.

"Seriously, you aren't hearing me. I need to talk to you," she said as he finally relinquished his power and prepared to hear her out.

"Okay, what's up?" he said, thinking that whatever it was, it had better be good.

"I took an assignment today with the Bureau to go undercover. I leave in two days," she said, bending her head down, not wanting to face him.

"Two days? Where you going?" he asked, as any normal person would.

"You know I can't tell you that," she said, holding true to her colors and her oath.

"There you go with that bullshit again. Well, when you coming back?" he asked, and waited for her response. She mumbled something but she was speaking so low he couldn't hear her.

"Speak up, I can't hear a word you saying," he said hastily, his temper ready to flare.

"I don't know when I'll be back," she said, still not facing him.

"How the fuck you don't know that?" He looked at her like she must be crazy if she thought he was going for that.

"Terrence, I'm an FBI agent. I'm going undercover, I will be back when my assignment is complete, that's all I know. I don't even know where they are sending me."

"Then how the fuck you know what you're doing if you don't even know where you're going?"

"I don't, I just know what the assignment is," she said—unfortunately.

"This is some real bullshit, some real fucking bullshit, man. I can't take this FBI shit. I told you before you needed to look for another job," he said, now pacing the floor, not liking what he was hearing.

"I know you ain't talking. If it wasn't for my job your ass would be in jail right now."

"That ain't the point," he argued.

"Baby, please, I really need you to understand. I'm just doing my job," she said, thinking about the photo of Angel Alvarez that Director Burns had shown her. Truth was Kimberly wanted the adventure. It was exciting and alluring, dangerous and deceiving. She would go away, pretend to be someone else, live another life, be a completely different person, and do whatever it would take to bring down her target, even if it meant compromising the values and principles of everyday life to do

so, even if it meant compromising her relationship with Terrence.

"I need to know if you'll be here for me when I get back,"
she said, tired of his ranting and raving.

"Shit, you don't even know when you coming back. How the
fuck you gonna ask me some dumb-ass question like that?"

"Terrence, stop crying like a girl and answer the question:
Will you wait for me or not?" she asked as she smookeyed him
with her body, pressing her firm breasts against him, reaching
her arms around his neck, intertwining her fingers, and kissing
the side of his face as she held him in her arms.

"Please, baby, I can't do this without knowing I got you back
here. I need to know that. I need to know I got something to come
back for—my man, my home, my life. Please understand."

"You asking a lot for a nigga to understand. It's not like you
even being honest with me, telling me what's going on. Shit,
to hear you say it, you don't even know what the fuck is going
on," he said, shaking his head.

"I know, baby, I know, but this assignment could really propel my career. I will be up for a promotion and a raise after this.
Please, I need you to be here when I get back, I need to know
you got me," she said, pleading with him, not realizing how
upset he would be.

"Go on then," he said grabbing her ass and stretching it
apart. "I'll be here when you get back."

"You gonna wait for me?" she asked, already knowing he
would stick his dick in a sheep to get off if necessary.

"Look, I said you'll have your home and I'll be here when
you get back, what more you want from a nigga?" he asked.

"I'll take that." She smiled as she held out her hand for him
to shake on it.

"You might as well, it's all you're gonna get," he joked, really serious, as he pushed her down on the sofa, deciding he'd better take advantage of her while she was still around. "Come on, let me get that," he said, roughing her up as usual.

Two days later, the time had come for Kimberly to report for her assignment. It killed Terrence to see her go, more than it bothered her.

"You gonna be all right?" she asked, realizing his tone was somber.

"Yeah, man, you be careful out there, wherever they got you going, ya hear?"

"Yeah, don't worry, I'll be back home soon," she said as she closed the trunk of her car, not wanting to spoil or interrupt his tender moment. She got into the driver's seat and started the engine, backed out of the driveway and put the car in drive, then put it in park, jumped out, and ran back to the doorway where he stood. She quickly hugged him and whispered in his ear.

"I love you."

Before he could start with his normal curses at her use of the L word, she ran away from him, back over to her car, hopping into the driver's seat and closing the door behind her.

I love you, too, he thought to himself as he waved back to her and watched her car fade away as she drove down the street.

Kimberly would be arrested for aggravated assault and prostitution. Her story was that she was a prostitute and had a john who got a little too drunk and a little too carried away. He started getting rough, beating her, trying to rape her, and during the struggle to defend herself, she hit him with a beer bottle, causing him to stumble and fall, busting the side of his head and cracking his skull. The john survived, but the charge of aggravated assault stuck and she was prosecuted and found guilty. She was sentenced to eight years in prison, eligible for parole in two to three. After being sentenced she was placed on a bus along with fifteen other women she had been in court with. Their destination was Federal Prison Camp Alderson, which was exactly where she was trying to be.

SERVIN' AND BIDDIN'

Kimberly entered the prison alongside the other women she had attended court with. Her new name in the system was Patrice Golden and her prison identification number was 32–786–45.

What if someone recognizes me?

That was her biggest concern, but Director Burns assured her that there was no one she would be serving time with whom she could possibly have come in contact with on the streets. But still, the thought of having her cover blown while locked up with serials and psychos had crossed her mind.

"All right, ladies, strip it down to your birthday suits. Search and sterile time," said a female correction officer, looking like Coach Balbricker from *Porky's*. She stretched her fingers in a tight plastic latex glove as she walked past the row of women, wiggling her fingers through the latex. "I'm watching you, ladies, all of you," she said, looking each of them closely up and down. She was always suspicious of the new intakes. They seemed to be the ones who thought they could beat the system and sneak some type of contraband or illegal substance into the facility—but not on her watch. "Let's go, put your clothes in the brown paper bag. When you're done, hand the bag over to CO Starks," she said, pointing to Starks, who was wearing a tan correctional uniform, her brown hair pulled back in a ponytail. "It is your job to make sure your name and number are written correctly on the bag if you want to ever see your clothing again. Remember, the next time you'll see your personal belongings is when you're going home, ladies. And for some of you, that's not going to be any time soon." She handed the intake sheet to Starks to initial for receipt of their belongings.

"How many lifers do we have today?" asked Coach Balbricker as she looked at her intake sheet over Starks's shoulder.

A tall, overweight black woman in her midforties standing in her birthday suit, second in line from the left, raised her hand.

"Well, listen here, 'Nothing to Lose,' the good news is just in case your sentence is overturned or by chance you strike it lucky on appeal, I'm going to save your things for you, too. Brown-bag it!" she snapped as she passed the brown paper bag to the woman, letting it drop on the floor.

Strip and sterile was the process of being inspected, sprayed, and sanitized, and to say the least, it was quite intense. There was nothing glorious about prison. There was nothing glorious about being locked away in a facility, and there was nothing glorious about having your everyday freedoms taken from you.

Afterward the girls were taken from intake to quarantine, where they would spend the first two weeks of their sentence in isolation. After quarantine, all the new inmates were allowed into population, assigned a block, a cell, and a bunk and normally, after two weeks in isolation an inmate would want to use the phone. It would take Kimberly some time to get settled into her new habitat.

"Here you go, home sweet home," said CO Starks, escorting Kimberly to her primary residence for the next three to five.

You got to be kidding me, said Kimberly, looking at her new living arrangements. *I thought I was getting my own cell,* she thought as she looked around her new living quarters.

It was tight, to say the least: a bunk, a toilet, and a sink. At the head and foot of the bunk were storage chests, one for each inmate in the cell. Her cellmate had decorated the walls with posters, and staring her dead-on as she entered the cell was an eighteen-by-twenty-four poster of the King himself, Elvis Presley. Everywhere you turned in the cell she had posters of Elvis. In the right corner of the left wall was a poster of Patsy Cline.

Is this really real?

Kimberly would be sharing a cell with a heavyset white woman with long, sandy brown hair and blue eyes named Lorraine Barker, who was serving a life sentence for murder in the first degree. Married off at the age of seventeen to William Barker, she had their first child one month later. Thirteen years and five kids after that, William had begun shacking up with Christine Wells across town, and when Lorraine found out that William was going to leave her and their kids for Christine, she went crazy, snapped out and killed him with a butcher knife in their kitchen while the kids were in school. Sad to say, she never really snapped back. And unfortunately, she was thrown into prison instead of a psychiatric facility.

"Jeepers, Starks," she yelled at the CO. "I thought you guys were going to tell me when I was getting a new roommate," said Lorraine as she hopped up and started straightening up the cell.

"No one has to answer to you, Barker, or tell you anything. You do as you're told or you'll see where you'll wind up," said the guard, ready to throw Lorraine in the hole if she didn't watch her tone.

Lorraine Barker had her dirty underwear and prison duds, as well as some of the toiletries she had just bought from the commissary, on the top bunk, and her bed wasn't made. The room was littered with pages that had been torn out of magazines and crumpled balls of yellow tablet paper.

"I pay her no mind. She's always so crabby," said Lorraine as she flagged CO Starks and then wiped her hands on her blue suit, holding her right hand out to greet Kimberly formally. "I'm Lorraine." She smiled, oh so happy to finally have someone to talk to.

"I'm Patti," said Kimberly, faking a smile.

"Oh, this is going to be so great. I haven't had a cellmate for quite some time, but finally, someone to talk to instead of myself," she said, kicking the balls of paper out into the middle of the floor's walking space.

"Nice," said Kimberly, as if she was Fabolous herself.

"I'm so sorry. I know it looks like a pigsty, but really, it's quite a charming cell when it's *Cleaned* up," she said, stressing the word *cleaned* in CO Starks's face as she swung around, grabbing her dirty underwear off the top bunk.

"Yeah, it's charming, all right," mumbled the officer, walking back to her post. "Charming as a troll's ass." She laughed to herself.

It didn't take Kimberly long to get settled in. It wasn't like she had major unpacking to do. She walked out of her cell and looked down the hall in both directions. It was busy, to say the least. Everyone had a job to do, everyone had somewhere to be, and those who didn't could be found chilling in their cells or in the television room and, of course, the phone station, where there were four phones per block.

Breakfast was served at 6:00 A.M., lunch was served at 11:30 A.M., dinner was served at 4:30 P.M., and it was lights out at 9:00 P.M. The prison offered the women commissary on Tuesdays and Fridays where they could purchase almost anything you could think of from tampons to Mounds and Almond Joy candy bars, as long as they had money in their accounts, or "on the books," as most referred to it.

"Hey, Bob Barker, how's that song go I like?" asked a Puerto Rican woman standing in the doorway wearing the normal blues, a red bandana around her head, and holding a toothbrush as she brushed her teeth and talked at the same time.

"Um, 'Crazy,' by Patsy Kline," guessed Lorraine, as if she would win a prize for the correct answer. She jumped up and began singing the song for her, just as crazy as crazy could be.

"Yeah, that's it." Angel smiled as she started singing it to herself before she walked back into her cell, right next door.

Get the fuck out of here, thought Kimberly positively identifying Angel as her target. *This is going to be easy, really easy.*

Or so she thought. Location had nothing to do with cracking the Angel code, 'cause Angel wasn't having it. She wouldn't even give Kimberly eye contact, and Kimberly did everything, everything that you could think of. She made it a point to leave her cell to eat breakfast, lunch, and dinner when Angel left hers. She sat as close to Angel as possible in the cafeteria or in the TV room. She worked out in the yard when Angel went outside. She said hello every time she walked by Angel's cell.

She even took a computer art class because Angel was signed up, but Angel wouldn't even look her way, let alone speak to her. Kimberly tried everything, even striking up small conversations in the shower about the latest news or weather, but Angel would just look at her, never saying a word. Kimberly could keep trying to fuck with Angel until the cows came home; it wasn't going to work. Angel had no intention of fucking with nobody in that joint. Her intentions were real clear: All she wanted to do was to win her appeal and get the hell out of there. She wasn't there to make friends with anyone, especially people who she didn't know from a can of paint. That was the last thing she had on her mind.

"Golden, you got a visit," shouted CO Starks down the block.

Kimberly paid her no mind, busy folding her uniforms and organizing her locker at the head of the bed.

"Golden, you got a visit. Hurry up before count," shouted the officer once again.

Lorraine looked at Kimberly sitting on the top bunk as if she had nowhere to go.

"Don't you hear the guard calling for you?" asked Lorraine.

"Me?" asked Kimberly, forgetting her last name was Golden.

"Yeah, you got a visit. She's been calling for you. Better hurry up before they start count."

"Oh, shit," said Kimberly, jumping off the top bunk. *I got to listen for my name, Patrice Golden, Golden, Golden,* she reminded herself.

"What took you so long," asked CO Starks.

"I was half asleep and I didn't hear you calling for me," she responded, all smiles. "I wonder who's here to see me?" she said, excited about her first visit.

"Oh, hold your wild horses, it's just your lawyer," said the officer.

Lawyer? I don't have a lawyer, Kimberly thought to herself, wondering who it could be.

Downstairs in the visiting room were four doors to four small nine-by-nine rooms. Each room had a table and two chairs. Kimberly sat in the room patiently, wondering what was going on. Just as she was about to get up and go back to the guard's station, Director Burns walked in, closing the door behind him.

"Director Burns, what are you doing here?"

"Counselor at law—call me counselor," he whispered, holding his pointer finger up to his lips, not sure who, if anybody, was listening.

Kimberly looked up at the ceiling, realizing they could be watched or wired, as he indicated.

"Counselor, I'm so glad to see you."

"So, how's it going?"

"Well, not really all that good, sir."

"Not good, why? I put you in a cell right next to her. How can it not be going good?"

"She won't talk to me. I can't get close to her at all."

"Are you serious?"

"Dead-ass, sir. She won't communicate with me. I've tried everything."

"It looks like we've got a real serious issue on our hands. The word is that a rival from a Dominican gang is looking to take Alvarez out; they're planning a hit on her."

"Are you sure?" asked Kimberly.

"One hundred percent, and our source on the inside said it looks like it's going down tonight. That's why I'm here, dressed in this suit, pretending to be your lawyer. You can't let them take her out; we need her alive. She's our only way to get at that Dutch character, who I personally cannot wait to get my hands on."

"What do I do?"

"Keep your eyes and ears open at all times, and don't let anything happen to Alvarez."

The director opened the door, finding a correctional officer in his face, standing less than two feet away. "And I'll get the corrected papers for you to sign," he lied as he smiled at the officer, waved, then walked away.

"Great," she said as the correctional officer led her out of the visiting area and into the back where she would be stripped, searched, then taken back to A block.

Walking down the hall she peeked into Angel's cell.

"What the fuck you lookin' in here for?" Angel spat at her.

"Oh, my bad, I was just looking for Lorraine," lied Kimberly; she was checking on Angel, making sure the Dominicans hadn't gotten hold of her.

"What the fuck you looking for her in here for?" Angel snapped, knowing Lorraine wasn't playing with a full deck and figuring neither was her new roommate, and that's why the institution had put them together in the same cell.

"You're right, why am I in here?" Kimberly said as if she was in a daze, and stumbled out of Angel's cell, leaving her alone. *She is mean as hell; this assignment isn't going to work at all.*

Dinner was at four-thirty and afterward the facility conducted a count of all the inmates. If they missed one person, they would have to start the process over again. Technically, by the time you ate dinner at four-thirty and did count, it was easily six-thirty, close to seven. Not to mention, the lights would be out soon, at nine-thirty. To say the least, it wasn't a lot of personal time. After count anyone who had a visit, wanted to shower, use the phones, or watch television could do so until lights out.

"Hey, Patty Cakes, guess what? It's Elvis night on *American Idol,*" screeched Lorraine. "I can't wait, can you?"

"No, I'm actually on pins and needles," Kimberly replied, playing along.

"Me, too."

"Uh-huh," said Kimberly, watching Lorraine humming to herself as she walked back out of the cell.

She got her shower bag together, her toothbrush, soap, and shampoo to wash her hair. She needed to get some underarm deodorant but kept forgetting to grab some at the commissary. She peeked into Angel's cell, on her way to the shower.

She was just in here. I wonder where she is.

Angel was in the shower, and a stall over was Rosalie, another inmate who had been on the block since Angel started her bid. Rosalie turned her water off and walked out of the shower room as three women wearing their blue prison uniforms walked by her.

"Hey, what are you doing in here? You not from this block," said Rosalie purposely, so that Angel would hear.

"Shut the fuck up and mind your fucking business," one of them hissed at her, threatening her, exposing a handmade wooden shank.

"Oh, my God," said Rosalie, bowing her head and turning away, not saying another word.

Just as Angel turned around to see who Rosalie was talking to, she saw Johanni, Eliza, and Morena turn the corner into the shower room. The Dominican women in the prison stuck together, and from the first time Angel set foot in FPC Alderson, they had vowed to take her out because, one, she was Puerto Rican and, two, she was a street legend. Eliza kicked in the shower stall door as Angel jumped back so that it didn't slam into her. It wouldn't have been so bad, but there were three of them. And when she looked down she could see Morena holding the wooden shank in her right hand. Eliza and Johanni weren't holding at all. Angel figured it was because they were the ones who would try pinning her down so Morena could stab her. She grabbed Eliza's head and dug her thumbs into her eye sockets as hard as she could, ramming Eliza's head into the tiled shower wall. Johanni quickly grabbed Angel, but her wet, naked body made her hard to hold. The water still running, Angel swung her around in a circle, trying to push her into Morena. But the wet tile caused her to slip and the two women fell to the floor. Angel bit into Johanni's hand, drawing blood, as Eliza picked herself up off the floor, blood pouring down the side of her face. She looked down at Angel rolling around on top of Johanni, kicking her ass, and as hard as she could, she kicked Angel, cracking three bones in her rib cage.

Angel screamed in excruciating agony as her body tightened. She rolled off Johanni, her naked body curled up in a ball, and that's when they went in, hard. All three women began stomping Angel's naked body. Her arms, chest, sides, head, and legs were being stomped just as Kimberly walked into the shower room.

"Hey, what's going on?" she asked as she saw Angel lying on the floor. "Get off her," said Kimberly, her first instinct to protect and serve.

"Mind your business."

"No, leave her alone, before I go get the CO and you end up

in the hole," snapped Kimberly, as if she would tell on them in a heartbeat.

"Coñaso, y quién se cree esta tipa que es? Hablando mierda de el hoyo de alguien! Yo te enseño el hoyo que tengo estúpida!" said Johanni, looking at Kimberly standing in front of them wearing nothing but a white towel.

"No lo sé pero ella se va a joder, eso esta seguro," said Morena, pulling out her shank and charging toward Kimberly with it as Kimberly fought her off, losing her towel. Angel lay on the floor unable to move, unable to get up, unable to speak, barely able to breathe. The cracked rib had punctured her lung, and her internal injuries were becoming life-threatening. She opened her swollen black eyes as best she could. Barely able to see, she watched as a naked Kimberly swung around and kicked Morena's head in midair like Chuck Norris. Morena's body dropped to the floor instantly. She did the same to Eliza and crushed Johanni's windpipe, instantly hitting her Adam's apple with a Shuto-uchi karate chop. Then she ran over to Angel, brushing the hair off her face.

"Oh, my God, are you all right?" she asked Angel, who wasn't responding. "Oh, please, God, please don't let her die, please." She felt her pulse; she was barely alive. Kimberly called for help, never leaving Angel's side. She cradled Angel's head in her lap and held her, brushing her hair lightly. "Can you hear me? It's going to be okay. They're coming for you, Angel. Don't worry, I won't leave you." And Kimberly stayed with her until help finally arrived and Angel was taken to the infirmary. Her injuries were so severe she was transported to the local hospital and returned five days later to the infirmary where she stayed for over one month.

Her first day back to the block, everybody cheered for her.

Word had gotten around the prison that Angel Alvarez was dead, and that Morena, Eliza, and Johanni had beaten her so badly that they killed her. She would be respected even more now that she was back on the block and had survived the attack. Morena, Eliza, and Johanni would be spending the next two years of their sentence in the hole, thanks to a phone call by Director Burns of the FBI. How dare they mess with his prime suspect? Anybody think of touching one hair on Angel Alvarez's head could kiss her ass good-bye. The Feds weren't having it, at least not until Angel led them to Dutch.

"Thank you," said Angel, standing in the doorway of Kimberly and Lorraine's Elvis-inspired cell.

Lorraine and Kimberly were playing a never-ending game of I Declare War with three decks of cards.

"Oh, wow, you're back, huh? How are you feeling?" asked Kimberly, standing to face her.

"Better, now—a lot better," said Angel, for the first time paying attention to all the Elvis memorabilia.

"Lorraine, you did all this?" asked Angel, staring around the cell in disbelief.

"Sure did," shouted Lorraine, peeking out from the bottom bunk. "Don't you just love him? He is the King."

Kimberly looked at Angel and twirled her pointer finger next to her head as she and Angel shared a moment.

"Can I talk to you?" asked Angel, leading Kimberly out of the cell.

"Hey, Alvarez, can't you see we got a very important game of I Declare War going on over here? Can't that wait?" asked Lorraine, not wanting Kimberly to go.

"Lorraine, I'll be right back." Kimberly smiled. "We can take a break. I been playing cards with you for four hours," said Kimberly, not realizing how much time had passed sitting around playing I Declare War with Lorraine in her Elvis love nest.

"I just wanted to really thank you," said Angel, staring at Kimberly face to face, examining her. She looked just like she remembered. "You know, a lot of people would have turned away, like Rosalie, and hauled ass out of there not saying a word. But you didn't. I probably wouldn't be alive right now if it weren't for you," said Angel, confessing a life's worth of gratitude.

Kimberly knew that this was her moment, her one and only chance to get close to Angel. All she had to do was play her cards right and she'd be on the top of Angel's list, the very top.

"You don't have to thank me," said Kimberly in a quiet, reserved tone.

"No, really I do. You don't understand, when I was lying there, I really thought they were going to kill me. I thought I was going to die. I never been stomped like that in my life. Are you kidding me? I couldn't even talk. I could barely open my eyes. I don't even know how I was breathing, but the whole time, I could hear you." She stopped for a moment, a tear in her eye. "I could feel you holding me, and rubbing my body, and it was like the whole time I was in the hospital, I could still feel you and hear you telling me I was going to be okay."

"I was so scared, Angel. I thought you were going to die. I couldn't leave you," said Kimberly, wanting Angel to really feel what she was saying, so she'd believe in her.

"How the fuck did you fight off big-ass Morena?" asked Angel, holding in a laugh.

"I don't know, that bitch is big. What the fuck? Where did she come from?" joked Kimberly.

"What is your name?" asked Angel.

"Patti Golden, well, Patrice, but everybody calls me Patti," she said, smiling at Angel.

"Angel Alvarez," said Angel, making a formal introduction and offering a handshake.

"I know who you are," said Kimberly enticingly, embracing Angel's hand, letting her know in that brief handshake, by not letting go, that she was down, completely down for her. "You don't have to tell me your name," whispered Kimberly.

"Yo, I saw you, like not everything, because I couldn't lift my head, but I saw you fighting them. You took them all down, singlehandedly, really quick, too. You was in there on some *Matrix* shit. Where the fuck did you learn that?" asked Angel, letting Kimberly know she had seen her fight game.

"I have a black belt in jujitsu."

"Wow, I always wanted to fight like that," said Angel, admiring Kimberly's body. "Seriously, though," she said, staying focused. "I really do thank you. I owe you. I owe you my life. Anything I got...it's yours. If you need anything, I got you," said Angel.

"Anything?" asked Kimberly provocatively, staring into Angel's eyes, letting her know that she wanted to make love to her.

"Anything," Angel answered back, as Kimberly pulled her shirt off and closed in on Angel, kissing her gently on the lips, finding their way to the bottom bunk and under Angel's blue blanket.

And that was how Kimberly Reese, special agent for the Federal Bureau of Investigation, got it in with Angel Alvarez and how the two fell in love on A block doing a bid. It was also the beginning of how she would eventually infiltrate Dutch's entire organization, bringing them all to justice, even Angel, or so she thought.

FREE AT LAST

Angel watched as Kimberly packed a box of her belongings and items she'd collected over the past two and a half years, then walked back into her cell. She couldn't stand to see her girl go.

"Wow, I wish I could make parole. Every time I go, they deny me," said Lorraine, hoping her luck would change.

"You will. Just be strong, Lorraine," said Kimberly.

Lorraine had caught a murder one charge for killing her cheating, constantly beating, and always drunk husband, William. And to this day she loved him with all her heart; he would always be the only man she'd ever be with for the rest of her life, not just because she was behind bars, but because he still held her heart, even in death. And she was sorry for what she did. It didn't matter, though: The parole board, psychiatrists, and other professionals had all rendered their findings. Everyone knew she was a borderline wacko nutcase with at least three personalities, and the penal system couldn't afford to explore the possibilities. The chances of Lorraine making parole were zero to none.

"It has been real nice having you for my cellmate. I'm really gonna miss playing cards, singing Sonny and Cher, and dancing to Elvis with you. You've been the best friend I ever had, and I've had like six other cellmates, and I'm telling you, you're like the best out of all of them," said Lorraine, bobbing her head, not wanting to cry in front of Kimberly.

"Aw, Lorraine, don't worry. I'll write you all the time and I'll get you some new Elvis posters and I'll find you a Patsy Cline one, too," said Kimberly, embracing her and rubbing her back.

Lorraine pushed her back. "Don't play, Patti Golden. Don't you play with me."

"I'm not playing. I will."

"Oh, my Jesus, please, thank you God. I've been so good, I've been doing everything right. Oh, my God, when do you think you'll get me the posters?"

"As soon as I can, okay?"

"Okay, you promise, and you'll write every week."

"Um...how 'bout once a month, okay?" asked Kimberly, not wanting to make promises she couldn't live up to.

"Okay, deal," said Lorraine, hugging Kimberly one last time. "I got to go if I'm going to get the phone, and I really want to call my aunt and talk to my kids. Don't forget to write," she said, missing Patti Golden already.

Kimberly peeked into Angel's cell. Angel was sitting on her bed, lacing a pair of sneakers.

"Hey, I just packed my box," said Kimberly, twirling one of her locks in her fingers. When she had arrived, she wasn't able to perm or straighten her hair, so she went au naturel and grew the locks. Now that she was going home, she had every intention of getting her hair done the way she used to before she went in.

"I can't believe you're leaving," said Angel, shaking her head, never picturing it ending like this. "I can't see me in here and you out there," she said, the reality throwing her sideways.

"I can always pick up another charge and be right back here. You want me to? I will, you know I will," said Kimberly, squirming up into Angel's arm, feeling her body next to hers as she reached between Angel's legs and gently played with her pussy.

"Naw, don't you dare. I need you out there more than in here," Angel said, knowing Goldilocks, as she had nicknamed her, was crazy and would be right back in her cell next week if Angel told her to. "If this fucking lawyer would come on, I would've been out of here."

"Okay, so don't worry about nothing. I got your lawyer information; I'll be on top of him. I got your books, so you'll be straight. Remember I told you about that little bit of inheritance money I got to go collect?" asked Kimberly, lying about where the money came from that she would use to flood Angel's books once she got out.

"Yeah, I just don't want you to go. I'm going to miss you," said Angel, not wanting to say the L word, as it was something that hadn't been said in their relationship over the past two years and a half.

"No, I'm going to freak out without you. I don't know if I can get through the day without being near you and touching you and making love to you, really. You're everything to me. You're all I got in this whole entire world. I don't want you to even look at another woman, you hear me?"

"Bitch, please, is you fucking crazy?" asked Angel, as if that would never happen.

"I think I'm going to cut my dreads now and just go with a short cut until my hair grows back," said Kimberly. "What do you think?"

"You could be bald. I don't care, I'll just call you Goldi," said Angel sounding depressed.

"See, that's why I can't live without you," said Kimberly, thinking of Terrence and how opposite he was to Angel. *I wonder if he'll be happy to see me.* There was only one way to find out, and she was on her way there.

Angel nodded as Kimberly walked by her cell carrying her box, being escorted by two COs down the row. She promised she'd write, she promised she'd catch each and every single one of Angel's calls every day, and she promised she'd take care of Angel's books until she got home. Whatever Angel wanted or needed, Kimberly would make sure she got it.

Kimberly thought of not waking up tomorrow behind bars. It had been a long two and a half years in prison. But she had done what she came to do: She had gotten in with Angel Alvarez, a top lieutenant in Dutch's criminal organization. The Bureau was absolutely positive that she would lead them to him, eventually. It might take them some time, but time was on the side of the government. As long as Agent Reese stayed in with Angel, there was no doubt that she would lead them right to Dutch. It was just a matter of time.

HOME SWEET HOME, PART ONE

Kimberly found Terrence exactly where he said he would be, but he hadn't kept his part of the deal like he promised. She got to their house, pulled up in the driveway, and began unloading luggage, piece by piece, and taking it up to the porch.

"What the fuck is you doing here?" asked Terrence, in his boxers, dick rock hard. All Kimberly could think about was how he would pull her, grab her neck, and tell her to bend over.

"How you gonna ask me that? I live here, remember," she said as she grabbed a piece of her luggage and walked past him. "Aren't you glad to see me?" she asked as they hugged each other.

"It's been two years," he stated, looking at her blankly.

"Well, look at it like I'm your army wife and I've been gone on my tour of duty. Now I'm home," she said, smiling, hoping he was still there for her, still wanted her, was still in love with her.

"I'm glad you're home. I missed you," he said hugging her

again. "Too long. Don't do it again, ya heard?" he asked her, meaning what he said.

"Wow, somebody really did miss me," she said, smiling.

"Shit, I ain't no goddamn windup toy." He was a man and he would do what he wanted. He kept his word, he was still there, she still had him, she still had her home.

But, no more—he had made up his mind. If she wanted to play cops and robbers that was fine by him, go on. But he wouldn't be sitting around making no more promises to a ghost. He understood it was her job, and that's why she needed to get a new one as far as he was concerned. If she left again, he'd tell her she had six months to get back home.

"I missed you. I really missed you," Kimberly said as she rubbed the side of his face.

"Stop playing. You know what you got to do coming through the door," he commanded, bending her over from behind. No kissing, no hugging, no foreplay, as usual—just straight Terrence, raw. She loved it.

The next day it was back to work. She had a meeting with the director and rushed to make it on time.

"Sorry, sir," she said as she walked through the door, after hearing him tell her to come in.

"Agent Reese. Good morning."

"Good morning, sir," she said as she sat down in front of his desk.

Director Burns praised Kimberly for a job well done. Her ability to gain access was remarkable, to say the least. He was more than pleased with the progress she had made. His plan now was to have both Roc and Angel released from prison before anything changed.

"So, how long before you'll have Angel released?" asked Kimberly.

"At least two months, maybe four tops, and she'll be out. Someone's hired very fancy lawyers and they've filed appeals. We're working on getting the appeals processed and granted. Once that's done, she'll be as free as a bird."

Kimberly sat thinking of what Terrence would say when she told him she'd be going undercover again. She knew he wouldn't be happy about it.

"Does Angel know?"

"Of course not. She won't find out until her appeal is decided on; that's what I'm working on now. In the meantime, you just do what you have been doing, 'cause it's really working," he said, convinced of her ability to penetrate the target. "I have a bank account for you, so if you need money, you have access to it, and lots of it. Write her letters, go visit her, put money on her books, stay connected—that's vital—and let the Bureau take care of the rest. You've been gone from home for two and a half years and you'll be leaving soon again once Angel is released."

"Don't you think I need to have a place to take her once she comes home?"

"Bingo. You need to be living somewhere, right, and a car?" he noted, approving a living expense budget for her. Director Burns left no stone unturned. "Okay, I think that's it. You'll hear from me once the judge is about to rule on the appeal. That way you'll have a little more notice. And Reese, excellent work out there," said the director, shaking her hand.

When Kimberly got the call from the Bureau that Angel was being released and it was time to start the operation, she had no idea how she would tell Terrence. Kimberly knew he was going to go ballistic. And he did.

"Again? You just came back! How long you gonna be gone this time?" he huffed at her, not wanting to hear it.

"I don't know, I can't make any promises. I honestly don't know," she said, hoping that he would understand.

"Well, I can't make any promises either," he spat back, pissed that he had spent the last two and half years alone, and she had finally come back merely to turn around three months later and say that she was leaving him again.

"Are you fucking serious, after eight years?" she said pushing him.

"You damn right. I'm tired of this undercover shit. If you cared about me, you wouldn't even ask me to go through that again. You been gone and now you're leaving again. Come on, shit ain't right. Fuck that, it's either me or that bullshit-ass job of yours."

"How can you even ask me to choose?"

"How can you even ask me to keep sitting around this motherfucker waiting for you to show up?"

"You know what, I can't stand here and argue with you. I have to go," she said, gathering her bags and carrying them out to her car. She went back inside, hoping that his demeanor had changed.

"I love you and expect you to be here when I get back," she said, embracing him and staring into his eyes.

"Come on, man. I expect you to be here tomorrow and tonight, like a woman is supposed to be there for her man. Oh…you don't know anything about that, I guess."

She wasn't going to argue with him, she wasn't going to challenge him, she wasn't even going to respond.

"I have to go," she simply said, letting her embrace go as she closed the door behind her, leaving Terrence alone once again.

HOME SWEET HOME,
PART TWO

Kimberly jumped out of the car and ran over to the gate as the security guards were letting Angel go. Angel had waived her right to a bus ride because she knew Goldilocks was coming for her.

"You cut your locks," smiled Angel, happy to see her lover and her friend waiting for her. "Damn, I missed you." She embraced Kimberly, squeezing her body tightly.

"Girl, I missed you, too. That was the longest three months of my life. I swear I thought I was going to go crazy. I'm so happy you're here," she said, hugging Angel once more.

The two left the prison as Angel looked back. *I understand why Dutch said he'd never return. Neither will I. Neither will I.*

"Baby, I got to get to California," said Angel, her wheels already spinning.

"California, why? What's there?" asked Kimberly, trying to figure out what Angel was up to.

"An old friend. You think we could drive out there?" asked Angel.

"We can do whatever you want," answered Kimberly, down for whatever.

"Can we do whatever I want right now?" asked Angel as she took her hand and slid it between Kimberly's thighs while she was driving.

"Can we?" asked Kimberly as Angel kissed her neck, fondling her behind the wheel. The two couldn't keep their hands off each other. It was actually the best sex Kimberly had ever had in her life.

Once they got to Kimberly's apartment, the two girls wasted no time. Kimberly stepped out of her sweatpants, revealing her firm, juicy ass to Angel's lustful eyes. She began to do a striptease for Angel, removing her shirt and bra slowly. Angel had enough of watching her and took her clothes off as Kimberly lay butt-ass naked on the bed. Angel took Kimberly's legs and placed them over her shoulders and went down on her as the two made love to each other as if back on A block. Lying next to each other, sweaty and wet, Kimberly stroked the side of Angel's face, looking into her eyes. "I love you," she whispered.

Angel rolled on top of Kimberly, pinning her down. In Angel's mind, if she said she loved her, then that meant Angel had her body and her mind.

"Would you kill for me?" Angel asked Kimberly, wanting to hear her answer to that.

"I'll do anything for you, Angel," she responded as Angel stuck her middle finger between her legs. The two began kissing and making love to each other all over again.

After two weeks of hearing nothing except, "I got to get to

California," Kimberly and Angel sat in the BMW outside the First Street Baptist Church.

"This is it—a church?" asked Kimberly. "You made us come all the way to California for a church?"

Angel began changing her clothes and started revealing exactly what they were there for.

"I won't rest until I know this motherfucker is dealt with. I just want you to blow the horn three times if you see someone coming or if I need to get out of there. Okay?" Angel asked, slipping on a blond wig over her head.

Kimberly watched as Angel walked up the street to the church in a tight silk dress and stiletto heels. She went around to the back, instead of up the steps. A few minutes later, Kimberly ran across the street, around the side of the church building to the back door. She peeked through a window. The curtain opened perfectly as she saw Angel mount the preacher and begin to fuck him. Kimberly watched as Angel took a blade and sliced the preacher's throat, blood splattering all over anything within its reach, including Angel.

Kimberly quickly ran back across the street, leaning back in the driver's seat as if she had been sitting there the entire time.

Angel slid her dress back down, walked out of the church office, and crossed the street to where Goldilocks was waiting for her.

As she got in the passenger side, she removed the blond wig, unpinned her hair, and shook it out to its full length. Goldilocks studied her. She had never seen this side of Angel before, but it was definitely the side she wanted to see. Goldilocks wiped the small spots of blood from Angel's face with a napkin.

I got you now, you crazy bitch, Goldilocks thought to herself with a devilish grin.

Angel knew after Qwan that Goldilocks was ready to ride or die for her no matter what. That made her smile. They pulled off and drove down the street, girlish giggles floating in the air in their wake.

Rahman lay on his back and looked at the bottom of the bunk over him. All he could think about was the *Don Diva* article and Angel. She said she had won her appeal. He knew she was probably out by now and he was certain he would go home soon, too. He had the perfect plan, but he couldn't help but wonder if he was ready for the streets again.

It was easy for him to be righteous in prison. But once freed, it was another story. He believed he had conquered his addiction. However, when faced again with the powerful calling of the streets, Rahman was weak to his obsession. He had made up his mind. He knew exactly what he was going to do when he was released, and no one would stand in his way, not even Angel.

TIME OUT

Rahman was escorted by two officers into the federal court-house in downtown Newark. He was there for his new appeal hearing and he couldn't have been more nervous. He looked behind him at his family. His wife, Ayesha, and their oldest two children were present. Rahman was advised to approach the judge so he could stand before him. He stepped forward. The judge never took his eyes off him. He just knew the judge was going to have it out for him. Rahman already considered his appeal denied.

"Mr. Rahman Muhammad. I see that you have filed another appeal in my court," the judge stated matter-of-factly.

"That is correct, Your Honor," Rahman calmly responded.

The judge opened the file that had been passed to him early on. It included a confidential FBI stamp and a note reading: *Request appeal to be granted for Rahman Muhammad. Part of ongoing federal undercover investigation. Will be under heavy sur-*

veillance. Association: Bernard James, Jr.—Essex Courthouse mas-
sacre and Month of Murder.

The judge had already spoken to the FBI director over the phone and made the deal to allow Rahman to be released. If it was up to him, he'd let Rahman rot in prison forever. The judge considered Rahman the luckiest man to walk in his courtroom in quite a long time. He closed the file and looked up at Rahman. Rahman swallowed hard as he awaited his fate.

"Mr. Rahman Muhammad, the court is granting your appeal and you are free to go," the judge stated.

Rahman couldn't believe it. Night after night he had dreamed of hearing those very words. Yet to hear the judge actually speak them brought tears to his eyes.

Rahman was now a free man, just like that. Ayesha grabbed him, hugging and kissing him, never wanting to let him go again. For close to three years he had been told when to eat, sleep, get up, wash his ass, and move. To have his freedom and basic human rights restored was truly a blessing. He vowed never to forget his ordeal and all he had endured. He vowed to never return to prison.

Rahman smothered his girls with tears and kisses, overjoyed to finally be reunited. But his wife, Ayesha, was who he had missed the most. She was his peace. Rahman promised Ayesha he would never leave them again. He had no idea that he was making a promise he wouldn't keep.

Rahman stayed true to his word about changing the streets of Newark for the better, while Angel was trying to get the streets the way they were before she had gone to prison. By the time he got out of prison and caught up with her, she was rockin' with Roll, a former rapper, now full-time hustler, who knocked Young World. Young World was Dutch's chosen heir to the throne. It was Dutch who had given Young World the dragon chain, passing down the reign.

Rahman knew Angel wasn't changing like he wanted her to, and when they finally ran into each other in the streets, he saw firsthand that they were on two different planes, heading in opposite directions.

"You can't win, Roc. You...can't win," Angel emphasized.

Rahman could win and he would win. It wasn't about drugs; it was about how the drugs were being sold, and how prevalent the drugs were in the community. That structure had to be changed. He wanted to change it, and so did his man Salahudeen, until Roll killed him. That was when Rahman knew he had to kill Angel. He tried, too, at the Newport Center Mall. Rahman shot at Angel, his bullet grazing her upper arm. She only made it out of the mall alive because Goldilocks came to her rescue.

"You missed me, Roc! But, I'm not gonna miss you!" were her last words as she made her escape

And of course she meant every word she spoke. Not long after Rahman attempted to gun her down, she rang his phone and let him know that she had taken a classroom full of first graders hostage at the Sister Clare Muhammad School and was going to kill them if he didn't turn himself in to her so that she could kill him. He knew his fate; still he chose to surrender himself. His wife, Ayesha, didn't want to hear it. She could care less how many children Angel held hostage, that had nothing to do with her and her family. Despite her pleas, Rahman had made his decision.

"No! No, Rahman! Wherever it is, whatever it is, no! You can't go!" she said, trembling, fearing the worst.

Ayesha was hysterical. Her instincts told her that something terrible was threatening to rip their lives apart. She didn't understand his choices, especially the choices he was making about his family.

"How could you do this to me, Rahman? How?" she whispered, looking at her children, who no longer had a father.

Nina looked in the mirror at the reflection of Dwight lying in bed under the covers, making slight breathing noises as he slept. He was a good man, a hard worker, loved the outdoors, played all sports, and had a real good job with an excellent benefits package. She looked down at the half-carat emerald-cut diamond he had proposed to her with. She had said yes at the time, but never should have. She wasn't in love.

I can't keep lying to him. I have to tell him the truth. The truth was she was still in love with Dutch.

She remembered like yesterday the day of Dutch's sentencing. She had avoided the trial, knowing she should have been there for him. And just when she thought he would be sentenced to prison for the rest of his life, she drove down to the courthouse only to find mayhem and mass confusion. The courthouse was on fire and the news reports came in that Bernard James was dead. She never got her chance to say good-bye. She wanted him to know she loved him, she'd be there, even if it meant waiting for him for the rest of his life.

Don't be a fool. It's hard to get a good man, and Dwight wants to settle down and have a family. Isn't that what you always wanted?

Nina had put in for a transfer at the bank she worked in to move to Maryland. The company was opening thirty new branches throughout the state and she was in line for a promotion, already serving as assistant branch manager. She had her sights set on Annapolis. She had always wanted to live near the water. A week ago she found out her transfer had been approved and a position awaited her if she wanted to take it. She thought long and hard about leaving Newark. It was a little intimidating to travel into the unknown, but she was ready to move on with her life. For the past couple of years she had been living in a twilight Dutch daze, completely stagnant. It was time to start fresh, time to rebuild her life.

She asked herself over and over again, trying to figure out why she couldn't commit to Dwight, the perfect man. *I'm so sorry, Dwight, I just can't.* She scribbled a note to him, breaking their engagement, on a piece of paper. When he woke, he'd find his ring placed neatly on the middle of the page. She tiptoed around the apartment gathering things she didn't want to leave behind and closed the door to what could have been her future behind her.

She thought of Delores, Dutch's mother, and their last conversation. Nina had pleaded with Delores to tell her if she knew anything about the rumors of Dutch's still being alive. The streets were always watching and always talking and word was that he had gotten away. But Delores refused to share her own secret thoughts about the body that she had signed for and had cremated. She had no choice but to keep her secret. She'd take it to her grave if she thought it would protect Dutch. Nina left Delores's house with a feeling that she was hiding something. No matter how much Delores denied knowing anything about the rumors, Nina saw right through her. *Maybe he is alive, maybe.* Nina felt it, and deep down, she believed that was why she knew in her heart she had done the right thing by letting Dwight go. *He deserves someone who loves him for him.* And that was how she rationalized the breakup.

She drove home in silence, listening to the crazy antics of Howard Stern, but not really hearing one word he said as her mind searched endlessly for the answers to her thoughts. She would make a "to-do" list of all the things she needed to accomplish in order to get through the transfer.

When she got home, she heard the faint sound of music playing, Rolls Royce, softly, like a whisper, coming through her living-room speakers. She looked at the receiver playing CD 2, track 12. Just as she was about to call the police and report an intruder, she realized this was the same song she and Dutch had danced to in the middle of the street so long ago. She looked down on the floor of the hallway leading to her bedroom. *What is that?* she said as she moved closer to a rose petal lying on the floor. A trail of rose petals continued to her bedroom door. Nina's heart was beating fast; the mystery of what awaited magnetized her. She wanted to call out his name but couldn't will her voice to work. She pushed the door open slowly, and what she found stopped her dead in her tracks. Her heart skipped a beat and she lost her breath as she read the rose petals sprawled across her bed.

Will you marry me? And below the question mark was a one-way ticket to Paris. Nina's body trembled as she listened to Nina Simone in the distance, knowing that it was him, it was Dutch, and he was coming for her.

"Yes, I love you," she whispered to the air, clutching the one-way ticket to Paris in her hand.

"Wow, I can't get over the two of you. I leave and come back...to this?" was the question Craze asked, as he looked at Angel about to kill Roc now that she had him where she wanted him, thanks to the little children of the Sister Clare Muhammad School.

"Cr-C-Craze?" Angel spoke in a hushed whisper as she lowered her gun. Angel's intention to kill Roc was immediately forgotten, and her beef with him was squashed, just like that. "Where's Dutch?" she asked. Craze laughed.

"Same ol' Angel...What? Craze don't get no love? Damn! What about me? Why you ain't been worried about ol' Craze?" Craze smiled, and Angel knew it was all good again.

She ran into his arms. He took the gun out of her hand and looked at Rahman, laying the gun down on the table.

"What up, Ock?" asked Craze.

"Long time no see," he said, thinking of how they had left him and Angel behind in prison cells to rot.

"I know, but it's all good. It took some time, but it's all good."

"A lot's changed since we last saw each other, Craze."

"Yeah, I see. You and Angel out this motherfucker trying to kill each other and over what? Look, Roc. You want Newark? Okay. It's yours. Every spot under Angel's control is now yours, right, Angel?" Crazed asked, looking at her, demanding a yes out of her mouth that very instant.

"Yeah, whatever, you can have it, Roc," she said, standing next to Craze. "You can have it all."

Rahman didn't say a word to either of them. He just looked at them, thinking back to yesteryear when they were all thick as thieves and the best of friends.

"I just got one question," said Craze, looking at Roc with steady confidence and surety. "What are you gonna do when the crooked cops, judges, the mob, and the cartels all come at you at once? Because you'll be eatin' off their plates if you stop the drugs in Jersey, especially Newark."

"Good point," whispered Angel over Craze's shoulder as she nodded in complete agreement.

"Don't 'good point' me, nigga! You so busy tryin' to take back what we left behind... We been there, done that, and now we've moved on, leaving the bullshit for the rest of the motherfuckers out here to kill theirselves over or end up sitting in a prison cell for the rest of their lives."

He gently lifted the dragon chain from her neck and held it up to watch it dangle in front of his eyes. He told her she should have buried it with Young World, then let it drop to the floor. Angel moved to pick it up but Craze stopped her.

"Leave it, Angel, just like we leavin' this petty street paper to the pawns who don't even know the game they're playing."

He turned back to Rahman. "You could have the streets, but the Feds would make sure you wouldn't keep them long. If you come with me, I'll really show you how to change the game. No more hood shit, no more street shit. We're international now, on some next-level shit." Craze smiled as the old Roc suddenly surfaced from nowhere and smiled back. "How 'bout it?" Craze asked.

Rahman realized Craze was right. Everybody from cops to district attorneys profited from drugs, either directly or indirectly. The whole criminal justice system relied on the backs of niggas and drugs; shit would never change. The hood would never rid itself of drugs. Who politically would even allow it to happen? Like Craze said, they both were fighting a losing battle. Rahman looked at Craze and asked him where they were going. Craze smiled, threw his arm back around Angel, and said, "We're goin' to see an old friend."

The three of them walked out, leaving the tangled dragon chain in a pile on the floor. To be forgotten for good.

ROLL OUT

Angel drove back to Goldi's apartment only to find it empty. *Where she go?* Angel wondered. She didn't have much, as she hadn't been home long, but the little she did have she began to sort and pack. She thought of leaving Goldi behind.

Damn, this shit is hard. I don't know what to do. She spoke to Craze about Goldi, assuring him that she was good peeps.

"Craze, listen, we did our bid together. She saved my life."

He heard her and he felt her pain; he didn't know what to tell her. Dutch was always game for another Charlie, and if Angel wanted the bitch to come, then who was he to shoot her down?

"Yo, she better be straight, man, that's all I got to say about it," said Craze, wanting to hear no more, putting the decision to bring her up to Angel.

Kimberly walked through the door. "Goddamn, it's hot out

there. When you get back?" she asked slipping off her tennis shoes.

"About a half hour ago," said Angel, her tone dull and her voice a little low.

Kimberly looked into the bedroom at Angel, who had a suitcase sitting on the edge of the bed. "What's going on? Why are you packing?" she asked

"I have to go. It's time that I leave," said Angel.

"Leave where?"

"Leave here, leave Newark."

"Well, should I get packed, too? I am going with you, right?" asked Kimberly, wondering if this was it. Was this the end?

Angel stared into Kimberly's eyes. Everything about Angel said to leave her, but she loved her; she wanted her along for the ride.

"Listen, this is the deal. If you roll out with me, that's it. There's no turning back, you understand? We're outta here. And there's no telling where we could end up because I don't know where we're going, but I know this much: We're never coming back. So, maybe you should think about it. Maybe going with me isn't the right thing for you. And don't let emotions guide you. I have to do this, and while I will miss you, I still have to handle my business. You never know—one day, once the smoke is clear and the dust particles are blown away, I might be back."

"Angel, please stop talking crazy. You can't leave me here. Bitch, I don't care where the fuck we at as long as we're together," said Kimberly, grabbing a suitcase, headed for the complete unknown but feeling one step closer to Dutch.

MIA

Delores stood speechless after listening to a message a woman by the name of Shirley Green had left on her answering machine. She had heard the phone ring but had refused to pick it up and decided to let the machine get it. Nurse Green said that she had a patient by the name of Bernard James, Sr., asking for her. *It can't be, not after all these years. I thought he died in the war.* If he's alive, why didn't he ever come back? Too many years, so much time, but her heart was still the same. The day he left was the day she watched love walk away and never return. *After all these years, he's here?*

She had to see for herself if it was him or some kind of mistake. She put her jacket on, grabbed her purse, and locked the door. She rushed down the steps and made her way to the bus stop, taking a seat on the wooden bench. She couldn't help but think of the first day she laid eyes on him. It was the summer of 1967 and her block was having its annual block party on a fine and sunny day.

"We ran out of hot dogs, sorry, Delores."

"You just told me to come back in ten minutes and they would be ready."

"Sorry, baby. They ate 'em already. You move too slow, Delores."

That's when she saw him, standing next to the grill waiting for the next round of hot dogs. He was tall and handsome, looking like Billy Dee Williams's brother. And the way he watched her was like a man starving for a woman. The only other thing she noticed about him was that he was a soldier wearing a green army uniform. The last time she had seen a soldier was when they invaded the neighborhood back in 1967 killing everybody who was outside rioting. Oh, she knew those uniform colors well. She saw firsthand how treacherous they were with her own two eyes. She remembered the tanks rolling down the street, soldiers with automatic weapons shooting at men and women caught rioting. That's why her first impulse was to get away from him. *How the hell can he even wear that damn uniform after what this government has done to us?*

Delores witnessed tanks of the National Guard rumble down the middle of the streets surrounded by soldiers carrying automatic weapons. The soldiers were shooting and locking up everyone they could. That's why Bernard initially drew her scorn instead of her interest.

So while she looked at him with disgust in her eyes, he looked at Delores in amazement. To him, she was the most beautiful girl he'd ever seen. He'd been around the world and back but hadn't found anyone that caught his eye the way she did. He knew he couldn't just stand there and let her walk away and not say anything to her.

Marvin Gaye's "What's Going On?" began to boom out of the DJ's speakers, and he knew right then he had to make his move, before somebody else did. He walked over to her.

"Hey there, mama, I say, what is really going on?" Bernard said, while Delores had her back to him.

Delores turned around and looked him up and down with feigned indifference—feigned because despite his uniform, he was fine. *Lord have mercy.*

"Why? You gonna arrest me or somethin'?" Delores asked with attitude.

Bernard smiled, showing off his pretty whites as he laughed. Delores was all of a sudden turned on by his voice.

"I might, if I can't get the next dance," he replied.

Right then, Delores's favorite song, "Victim" by Candi Staton, came on. She knew she wanted to groove to it with him, but instead, she folded her arms across her chest and looked away.

"I don't like this song."

"Come on, sugar. You expect me to believe that when your body is sayin' something else?" he said as he watched her move to the beat.

Delores smiled, letting him know he was right.

"You know, I've been around the world twice and had every flavor there is, but ain't nothing like you ever come 'cross my plate."

She looked him up and down again, but the truth was he had her open, just like that, and her heart had already been softened by his sleek charm. She knew she was being gamed, 'cause she was the queen of game. Yet still, she liked it. She then smiled, appeased to know she was being judged by worldwide standards.

"Ah, she smiles. So, now, can I have your name?" Bernard smiled, knowing he was in there.

"No," Delores stated simply.

"No?" he questioned her back, wondering who she thought she was talking to.

"No, but you can have this dance," she said, looking into his eyes.

He grabbed her hand and led her to the middle of the street, where everybody was getting their groove on. Song after song, they moved as if they were dancing on clouds in the sky to a rhythm of one heartbeat. For thirty days and thirty nights they danced the same beat, making passionate love to each other as if neither had a care in the world. Then on the thirty-first day, like a ticking clock, she walked into the room as he was looking out the window on what seemed like one of the rainiest days of the year.

"Baby, you okay?" Delores couldn't help but be worried by the expression on his face.

"If there was anything I didn't plan on for this leave, it was to meet someone like you."

"Leave?" *What does he mean by leave?*

"Leave days. My tour of duty ended and after that you get a thirty-day leave. Most people don't call it a leave, but I do."

Delores couldn't speak. Her mind spun like a top set loose, whirling and whirling around and around.

He can't leave me. Please don't leave me. How could he do this to me? I thought he loved me. These were her thoughts as he walked over to her.

"I—I ... I know it's hard to hear, 'cause this is hard for me to say," he said with tears in his eyes and a pained look on his face, as if his world was more torn than hers. "And I know it'll be even harder to do, but you see, sugar, it's something I gotta do." He tried to explain to her his mission, where he was at as a man in this world. And even though she didn't want to, Delores understood his reasoning. She knew deep inside that he wasn't telling her he was leaving, he was asking her to let him go, and she couldn't get in the way of his doing what was in his heart to do.

Her last words to him were, "I love you," as they parted ways at the train terminal. That was the last she ever heard or saw of him. He never wrote and he never came back. Three weeks later, she missed her period and found out she was pregnant. She never had the chance to tell him. Nine months later, she had the baby, a boy, and named him after his father, Bernard James, Jr., but the world would know him as Dutch.

Delores arrived at the VA hospital thirty minutes after the call from Nurse Shirley. She went to the reception desk and was handed a visitor tag and given the room number. She peeked in. Bernard was lying still, his eyes closed, asleep.

"Are you Ms. Murphy? Hi, I'm Nurse Green," the nurse said, smiling at Delores. "He's asleep now, but he comes and goes. If you'd like I can wake him and let him know you're here."

"No, no, let him sleep. I can wait," Delores said as she walked into the room and took a seat by the bed.

"Let me get you a fresh container of water and some ice chips," said Nurse Green, hurrying out of the room to fetch everything.

Delores sat by the bed looking at the man whom she had wished for all her life. She touched his hand, her fingers needling their way between his, and she squeezed his hand tightly as he opened his eyes and looked at her.

"Delores." He smiled.

"Yes, Bernard, I'm here," Delores spoke softly, reassuring him with comfort. "Go on and rest. I didn't mean to wake you," she said, looking into his eyes, wanting to know why he never came back for her.

"They done caught me, Delores. You got to get me out of here," he said, now worried half to death.

"Bernard, ain't nobody caught you. You are in the hospital. Don't worry. I won't let nothing happen to you."

"You gonna get us out of here?" he asked as if it was mission impossible.

"Of course. Don't worry about that. You just get your rest." Delores smiled, figuring he was suffering from dementia.

"Delores."

"Yes, Bernard."

"I missed you in my life...I missed you in my life," he repeated, wishing he had one last chance to do his life over again.

"I missed you, too."

She fell asleep in the chair next to his bed awakening to deafening screams.

"Brigade attack! Incoming, one, two—get down, get down!"

Nurse Green ran into the room. Delores didn't know what to do. Bernard appeared to be awake because his eyes were open, but actually, he wasn't. He was having a nightmare.

"It's okay. We're here, we're right here," said Nurse Green, awakening Bernard from a deep sleep as she rubbed his chest and arms, talking him out of the nightmare he was in.

He opened his eyes, looked around the room, then stared into the eyes of a smiling Nurse Green. "Aw damn, I been caught," he said, looking at the white woman.

"You're not caught. You're right here." She chuckled, patting his shoulder. "What am I going to do with you, huh?" she asked him, as if he was joking. "That's what he always says when I wake him up from his nightmares," she said, speaking to Delores as she held a cup of water for him to sip from a straw.

Delores looked on, realizing this wasn't dementia, this was something else.

"Can I speak with you?" Delores asked, moving away from the bed. "What's wrong with him?"

Delores wasn't a medical professional, but then again you didn't need to be to tell something was off about him, really off.

"He has kidney failure, sclerosis of the liver, high blood pressure, and post-traumatic stress disorder."

"Post-traumatic stress disorder?" questioned Delores, not sure what that was.

"From the Vietnam War, when he served," responded Nurse Green. "He's suffering from a nervous breakdown, and he's to the point where he can't take care of himself."

Delores thought back to yesteryear and the strong, tall, handsome soldier she remembered from her dreams.

"We would have transferred him to a mental facility but his blood pressure was high when he was admitted. When I told him that he was going to be transported to a facility in Trenton, New Jersey, that could care for him, he asked me to call you. So, I went on the Internet yellow pages, looked you up, and called. If you're not willing to take him and sign him out, I'll be transporting him to Bellevue once his vitals are stable."

Bellevue, thought Delores. She knew if they were shipping him to Bellevue then he wasn't mentally stable at all.

She went and sat by the bed, once again taking his hand in

hers. He turned his head toward her as if seeing her for the first time.

"Delores...It's you," Bernard said, hardly able to talk, he was filled with so much emotion.

"Yes, I'm here," she said realizing that he didn't remember an hour ago. *Oh boy,* she thought to herself.

"Delores, please, please, they got me. Please, Delores, please get me out of here. Please don't let them take me, Delores. Don't let me die here," he begged her.

"Don't worry, I won't let them take you nowhere and you not dying no time soon. You coming with me, Bernard. You're coming home with me."

She looked at his nurse. "You can go ahead and get the papers ready. I'll sign for him," she said, positive she was doing the right thing. Delores didn't have to give it a second thought. There was no way she would leave him behind, no way she'd let them lock him away in a facility for the mentally ill. She had no choice. She had to take him with her. Now, after all these years, he would finally be home, home where he belonged, with her.

NINA TIME

Paris, France

Nina arrived in Paris, touching down one day before Craze, Angel, and Rahman. Craze had previously made arrangements for her, knowing he wouldn't be there when she landed. Nina followed the signs to baggage claim holding a Rosetta Stone translation booklet in her hand. A man wearing a black suit with a white shirt and black tie was waving a sign that read Nina Martin. She smiled, walked toward him, and introduced herself.

"Hello, how are you?" he asked in his native language.

Rosetta Stone ready, she responded, "I am well, thank you."

"Do you have luggage?" he asked as she stared blankly, not remembering that line from her studies.

He pointed to the baggage belt and asked her again.

"Oh, yes, luggage." She smiled as she walked over to the belt.

The driver got her bags and opened the door to the black S600 Mercedes for her to get into the back passenger seat.

"Thank you," she said as the door closed behind her. An envelope marked "Nina" sat on the seat next to her, as did a single rose. She opened the envelope, reading the card; "Dinner."

The driver pulled into the Hôtel de Crillon where she was booked in a suite on the fifth floor. A doorman opened the car door and assisted her exit.

"Welcome, madam. The front desk is through the door and to the left," the doorman said as he began taking the luggage from the driver.

"How much do I owe you?" she asked the driver in English, forgetting she needed to speak in French. "Oh, I'm sorry," she said, repeating her question in French.

"It's already taken care of, thank you, and enjoy Paris. It is a very beautiful and very romantic city."

"Thank you," she said, passing him a tip before making her way to the front desk. She approached the front desk manager, giving him her driver's license and credit card.

"Do you have luggage?" he asked in his best effort at English.

"Yes," she responded, letting him know she had a little continental etiquette.

"Franco, can you take Ms. Martin's bags to her room, please? She's in the penthouse suite. This will not be necessary. Your room is completely taken care of," he said, smiling and passing her back her driver's license and credit card.

"Oh, thank you," she responded, the words "completely taken care of" ringing in her head.

"Here you go," he said, speaking in French and dangling a key chain between his thumb and pointer finger. "You are booked in the Bernstein Suite. This is the key to turn the elevator lock. After you unlock it," he said, sticking the key into the air and turning it to the left, "press 5." He smiled using his pointer finger to press nothing. "Make sure you lock it again," he said, turning the key back the other way, "so only you have access to the floor." Then, in English, he asked, "Do you understand?"

"Yes, elevator key," she said, waving the key in the air as he just had. "Room key, right?" she said, acknowledging the other key.

"Very good for you. Enjoy your stay with us."

I plan to. I really do. Nina smiled as she strolled across the lobby and took the elevator to the fifth floor. The double doors acted as the doorway, and stepping inside the suite was like slipping into a fantasy, an enchanted, traditional, lush, and lavish fantasy world filled with the finest china, silver, tapestries, furnishings, floor coverings, chandeliers, painted cathedral ceilings, and true-blue Egyptian linens. She felt like Mary Antoinette, the queen of France. *So this is eating cake?*

The telephone rang and the thought ran through her, *Dutch, it's him.*

"Hello," she said, answering the phone before the second ring.

"Good evening, madam, my name is Alfred and I am your evening butler. I want to make sure your stay with us is most enjoyable. Do you need my assistance?" he asked in a twisted but understandable English.

"Umm..." Nina thought for a minute if she needed anything. "I would like some water," she said, hoping it wasn't too much to ask.

"Right away, ma'am, right away."

He dropped the line and in less than forty seconds Nina heard a knock from a side hallway door that led to the butler's chambers.

"Good evening, Miss Martin," he said, greeting her in his native French, as he walked through the door she held open for him.

"Good evening, sir. Thank you," she replied, accepting the water from him.

He stood vigil, as if he were not just a butler, but a keeper of sorts. "I have been instructed to give you this, a gift from Mr. James."

"A gift?" Nina questioned, taking the red-gold-trimmed Cartier box from her butler's hands.

She opened it, looking at the twenty-carat aquamarine-colored stones trimmed in carat-cut round diamond earrings along with a matching diamond necklace containing one large aquamarine stone that dangled on her chest.

"Oh, my..." Her breath escaped her and she thought she might faint. Tears came to her eyes. "I've never seen anything so beautiful in my life," she said, covering her mouth in sheer amazement.

"Rachel had these flown in from New York today. They were actually delivered an hour ago. I haven't had time to take them out of the boxes." He smiled as he placed four boxes containing four exquisitely designed evening gowns next to her.

"Rachel?" Nina asked.

"Rachel Roy and I think you will find them..."

"This is the most beautiful gown I've ever seen in my life," Nina interrupted, gazing at the baby-blue silk gown, lightly beaded, trimmed, and absolutely stunning.

"She was instructed to design them for a princess."

"Really?" Nina stopped, looking up at him, opening another box.

"Yes, of course." He smiled knowingly, because he was the

one who had given the instruction to Rachel himself. "The car will be here to pick you up at six o'clock. Are you sure you don't need anything else?"

"No, thank you. Thank you so much."

"Of course. Let me get your stylists for your hair and your makeup—we don't want you to be late," he said before leaving the room.

Nina was speechless for the first time in her life. She had never imagined that her dreams could come true. But today one of them had. She looked at the diamond necklace and earrings, the Rachel Roy originals, then around the vast penthouse suite designed for a queen and king. *All this. He didn't have to do all this*, she said to herself, thinking of Dutch and how beautiful she wanted to look for him. Nina was happy and excited at the prospect of seeing Dutch, anticipating the entire evening. Bathed, dressed, primped, and completely assisted, she swooshed out the door and stepped onto the elevator, facing Alfred, Marceline, and Josée.

"Have a wonderful time. You look absolutely beautiful. He will love you," said Josée, the hairdresser who had swept her hair up, leaving dangling strands lying perfectly, on the side.

"Yes, absolutely beautiful. He won't be able to resist you," said the girl who had done her makeup as she blotted the side of Nina's face, touching her up in the elevator light.

"I feel like Cinderella."

"You are more Cinderella than she herself, except you don't have to worry about the stroke of midnight."

A driver was waiting for her and quickly swept her inside the car and down the street. He drove to the Seine's waterfront, where a private sixty-foot yacht was waiting for her to board.

She boarded the yacht as a servant assisted her, handing her a glass of champagne.

"Thank you." She smiled as Dutch emerged from inside and walked toward her. He looked like the million-dollar man, wearing a black tuxedo. A classical quartet played in the background near a candlelit table decorated with the finest china. Their eyes locked, and in that moment, everything that hadn't been said was finally spoken.

Nina ran to him, enfolding him in her arms. "I missed you so much," she said, looking into his eyes. Their lips found each other's as they gently kissed.

"I missed you, too," Dutch said, looking into her eyes.

"Dinner is served," said a butler, followed by two servers who pulled chairs from the table for Dutch and Nina to be seated.

The dinner was fabulous. Their menu consisted of Cajun crusted rib-eye with fresh blue cheese cream, alongside apricot chicken marsala, curried rice with shrimp, Portuguese-style collard greens, and sweet cream cornbread. The two talked and danced and shared the past three years.

Of course she needed him to know that she had a change of heart and was rushing to see him at the courthouse, but was too late. By the time she had gotten there it was a fiasco—commotion from the police, the news reporters, and then the courthouse catching fire, and finally came the news reports that he was dead.

"I came, you know. I was there that day, but you were gone and they said you were dead and...all this time all I wished was that I had gotten the chance to tell you," she said, fading off, not quite completing the sentence.

"Tell me what?" he asked, wanting to hear what she had to say.

"I wish I had gotten the chance to tell you how much I love you," she confessed, looking into his eyes, telling him the God's honest truth.

"I hope you mean that, because I wouldn't have you here if I didn't think you did."

Dutch played no games and had no time for bullshit. It was then he told her how Craze had helped him escape from the courthouse, how Mr. Odouwo got him safely out of the country, and about his new business dealings with the Odouwo family and the diamond trade. It all made sense to Nina, everything he said helped fill in the missing pieces of all that she had wondered over the past three years.

"Why didn't you call? Why didn't you come back for me sooner?" she asked, wishing that he hadn't stayed away for so long.

Truth was he wanted to. But with Nina, there was no telling. What if she didn't come? What if she didn't want him? He couldn't risk playing games in the States. The stakes for him were too high.

Dutch didn't answer her, but rather closed in on her, wanting his body next to hers. He kissed her passionately, holding her neck as his hand slid down her back, his fingers unzipping her gown. Nina had been waiting for this moment for three years. She had dreamed him and felt him thousands of miles away and now, finally, here she was with him. They took off each other's clothes, and as Dutch gently lay on top of her, their bodies combined together as one.

"I love you, Dutch, I love you," she cried, as Dutch made passionate love to her until both collapsed into a deep sleep.

Nina awoke the next morning to find herself alone. She rolled over and immediately sat up. She saw Dutch standing shirtless on deck looking out at the river. She wrapped her naked body in a sheet and went outside where he was.

"How did you sleep?" he asked her as he extended his arms for her to come to him.

"The best night's sleep ever," she said as Dutch embraced her. "Are you hungry?"

"Yes I am."

He spoke in French, ordering breakfast to be served.

"We are headed back to the dock, where a car will be waiting for us," he said, thinking of Craze and hoping he had had a safe return to Paris. "But, before we go, I need to ask you something."

"What?" she asked, ready for anything.

"I need to know that it's all or nothing between us no matter what."

"Of course, I love you," she responded. "I'm here because I love you. I don't care what hard times we have to go through."

Dutch hoped and prayed she meant every word that she spoke, because there was no turning back, no changing the game in the ninth inning, and no time for uncertainty. It had to be what she said it was: love.

UP AND AWAY

Rahman, Angel, and Goldilocks waited inside the plane as Rahman kept an eye out the window.

"Here he comes," said Rahman, watching Craze's car pull up next to the boarding steps.

"What took you so long? I thought something happened to you. Where's Dutch's mom?" asked Angel, standing up as Craze boarded the plane, her questions flying at him a mile a minute.

"You're not going to believe it," he said, smiling, still reeling from his visit with Dutch's mother.

Craze sat down next to Rahman and put on his seat belt, and as the plane moved across the runway for takeoff he told them of meeting Dutch's father.

"Who is it?" Delores asked, looking out the peephole at a bearded old man in her hallway.

"It's me, Chris," he said, tipping his hat so she could see he was dressed in costume, already knowing the white van parked down the street was the FBI watching and waiting for Delores to lead them to Dutch.

"Boy, if you don't get in here . . ." She began to cry. She slammed the door behind him, hugging him as tightly as if he was her own birth son. "Where you been? Where's Dutch? Is he okay?"

Delores had a hundred and one questions, and as she rambled, still standing in the doorway, Craze could see an elderly man lying down in Delores's bedroom.

"Who's that?" he asked, as if he were a jealous lover.

"You won't believe it," she said, full of smiles. "It's Dutch's father. He's real sick, Craze—he's not doing too good. The doctors said he had sclerosis of the liver and don't expect him to live much longer. So, when he asked me to take him home and get him out of the hospital, I did."

"Does Dutch know?"

"Nope, and neither does his father," she said, staring off into the distance.

"What do you mean? He doesn't know he has a son?"

"No, I haven't found the right moment to tell him. But I will. I will."

Craze walked into the bedroom and looked down at the man Delores claimed had fathered the all-time legend, Dutch, himself.

One thing was for certain and two things were for sure: Dutch was the spitting image of the man.

"Wow, Dutch looks just like his dad," said Craze, wishing he knew who his father was.

"Yeah, just like him." Delores led Craze back out into the living room. "So, what in the world are you doing with yourself?"

"I came to get you," said Craze. "Take you back to where Dutch is."

Delores drifted off into silence, thinking of the last three years and how many times she had prayed to God for the chance to see her son just one more time.

"I can't. I can't go. I can't leave Bernard. I promised him I would take care of him. You should have seen him begging me not to leave him with them white folks in the hospital," she said, laughing at the thought. "I can't leave him now," said Delores, making one of the hardest decisions she had ever made in her life.

"I understand. Don't worry, I'll be back for you again." Craze smiled embracing her shoulder and kissing her cheek.

"I've been worried sick. I'm glad to know he's all right. I'm so glad I don't have to worry."

"No, Dutch is good. We're all good. Just take care of his dad and look out for old men with long beards," joked Craze, gesturing at his homeless-man costume with its funny hat, long beard, and mustache.

"You just keep your head up, baby, and don't let them catch you guys, you hear? Don't let them catch you, Craze," she said, hugging him and kissing the side of his face.

"Oh, shit, I almost forgot to give you this. Dutch wanted you to have this," he said, passing her something wrapped in a brown paper bag.

"What is it?" she asked, taking the brown bag from him.

"Just a little to hold you over until I see you again," he said as he waved good-bye to her just before the elevator doors closed.

Delores waved good-bye and shut her apartment door. Relieved was the word to best describe how she felt. She walked into the kitchen, sat down at the table, and looked into the bag. She counted out half a million dollars, three stacks of nothing but hundreds, wrapped in a grocery bag. *He is alive. I knew he was.* Her heart skipped a beat. She smiled and closed the bag.

Paris, France

Goldilocks couldn't wait to see Dutch with her own eyes and finally get him and his team into FBI custody. She smirked at the thought of how slick she had been. Technically, she was winning. She threw Angel off three years ago when they were back in jail. And the whole time they had been together, nothing ever threatened her relationship with Angel. The relationship was smooth sailing, and now it would only be a matter of time.

There were two black, bulletproof Cadillac Escalades waiting for them when Mr. Odouwo's private jet touched down at Paris's Charles de Gaulle Airport. They arrived at the Hôtel de Crillon. Craze had had one of the Charlies take care of booking the room a few days in advance.

"We're all on the same floor," Craze said, passing a room key to Angel and one to Rahman. He wondered how Dutch and Nina were making out. He looked at his watch.

"We're gonna meet up in about an hour with Dutch. Until then, I'll be in my room chilling if you need me," Craze said, giving Rahman a handshake good-bye, before slapping five with Angel.

Goldilocks couldn't believe it. In one hour she would be able to make a positive ID and alert the FBI. It was just that simple. At the rate she was going she'd have Dutch behind bars before midnight.

"What you smiling 'bout?" asked Angel, looking at Goldilocks, who was lost in her reverie.

"Oh...nothing, just happy we're here. Do you believe it?" she asked, diverting Angel's question as they walked down the hall to the elevators. Goldi burst through the door as she opened it. "Wow, look at this place," she said, spinning around in Angel's arms.

"Shit's crazy, right?" Angel asked, letting her go as she opened a door to the bathroom. "Damn, they gots the marble caked up to the ceiling in this chumpy."

"Yeah, this place is beautiful. I'm so glad you brought me," Goldilocks said, wrapping her arms around Angel as she began kissing her neck. Before either knew it their clothes were a trail from the bathroom to the bed. Not until Craze knocked at the door did Angel realize that an hour had passed.

"Shit," she said, hopping out of the bed and throwing on her clothes. She opened the door and peeked out.

"What up?" she asked.

"It's time to go. Why you look like that?"

"Okay, wait a minute, let us get dressed," Angel replied, trying to close the door.

"Hold up, ain't no us with that broad," said Craze, letting Angel know to keep her broad in her place.

"No problem," said Angel, knowing she couldn't argue with Craze and win on it. She nodded, closed the door, and proceeded to get dressed.

"It's time to go?" Goldilocks asked, ready to get dressed, too.

"Naw, B, you gotta stay here. It's just the family tonight."

"So I can't meet Dutch?" Goldilocks asked, irate.

"What you worried about meeting that nigga for? You wanna fuck 'em or something?"

"Hell no. I just didn't expect to be by myself, that's all. You know I don't want no dick on my plate."

"You better not. That's my pussy, you heard?" Angel asked, pulling her close and kissing her on the forehead before she left the room.

Goldilocks sighed a breath of relief as she closed the door behind Angel. *That was close,* she thought, realizing showing any sign of interest in Dutch around Angel wasn't a good idea. *Damn, I wanted to ID this bastard. I'll get him. It's just a matter of time. He can run, but he can't hide.*

Goldilocks threw her jacket over her shoulders. Tonight would be the perfect opportunity to sneak away and make contact. *I know they are wondering if I'm okay.* She walked down the street and turned a few corners, eventually finding a pay phone outside a tiny café. She swiped a call card and phoned in to her commander.

"Commander. This is Agent Reese."

"Agent Reese, state your location."

"I'm in Paris, sir."

"Paris—Paris, France?"

"Yes, sir."

"Have you been able to confirm that Bernard James is alive or have you made contact?"

"No, not yet, sir. But I will very soon."

"Agent Reese, the sooner you can determine that Bernard James is alive the quicker we can take him down."

"I understand, sir."

Goldilocks hung up the pay phone, terminating the call. That was when she noticed a white van with dark-tinted windows parked across the street. Then she noticed three men walking on the opposite side of the street. She started walking down the street and quickly turned the corner. She turned around only to see the three men still following closely behind her. Goldilocks knew exactly who they were. She dipped into an alleyway, hid herself in a sunken doorway, and waited.

"Why the fuck are you here? You should have never followed me here! You better hope you didn't blow my fucking cover!" Goldilocks yelled to the field agents.

"What the fuck are you doing out here by yourself anyway? Do you think you're sightseeing? You're supposed to be finding James," Agent Shipp quipped.

Agent Shipp had originally been assigned to go undercover, but it was felt that Agent Reese would be a better match for Alvarez. Shipp wanted Dutch just as badly as Goldilocks, but he didn't want to see Reese be successful in bringing him down. If he had it his way, he'd remove her altogether.

"I am finding James. I certainly didn't follow you here," she said sarcastically.

"Goddamnit, Reese. If I were leading this case I would have had James's ass expedited back to the States yesterday. You're starting to look like a damn rookie again out here."

"You wouldn't have done shit! You know what? If it wasn't for me, Bernard James would still be a mystery to everyone. I'm going to be the one who brings Bernard James in whether you like it or not."

"Well, you need to do it, and do it quick, fast, and in a fucking hurry, or you best believe I'll be popping my fucking head back up your ass again. You got that, Goldilocks?" Agent Shipp said, leaving the hint of a threat in the air.

"Fuck off, asshole," she mumbled as she watched him and two other agents walk back down the street.

Agent Reese hated Shipp's arrogance. For years, the two had had a hate-hate relationship. But if he thought for one minute that he was going to bust her bubble, he was wrong. She had gotten this far without any help from the Bureau. She certainly didn't need it now, and she certainly didn't need Agent Shipp. *Who the hell does he think he is? I already got Dutch. It's just a matter of time.* Goldilocks left the alley and went back to the street and blended in with the crowd.

DUTCH MASTER

Craze took Angel and Roc across the Seine in a small speed-boat and down the same trail Nina had walked the night before. Dutch waited under the canopy of a cottage with three Charlies watching his friends arrive from a distance. As soon as Angel saw Dutch she couldn't help but run to him.

"Dutch!" she yelled, still not believing that it was really him. She ran into his arms. Angel embraced him tightly. She didn't want to let him go.

"I can't believe it. It's you, it's really you," Angel said, full of smiles.

"You all right?" he asked, happy to see her again.

"I am now," she answered.

Roc walked slowly, taking his time. He had mixed emotions on seeing his friend, since he was still battling his own demons. Dutch looked over Angel's shoulder and smiled at the sight of Roc. He let Angel go and embraced Roc.

"I miss you, my brother," Dutch told him.

"I miss you, too."

Roc held Dutch, taking it all in. Flashes of their lives, intertwined, and all the years of getting money, committing crimes, and putting in work reminded Roc just how much love he had for the man. He knew the forces of evil and the forces of good. He was and wanted to be a good Muslim man, but there was only a thin line between his faith and his reality.

"How's your wife and the kids?" Dutch asked.

"We not together no more," said Roc solemnly.

"Damn, I'm sorry, man. You all right?"

"I am . . . now," Roc said, letting go of all guilt and all demons as he smiled at Dutch, thinking of all they had been through together—and now here they were, side by side just like old times.

"Come on, come on inside," he said, giving Craze a pound and holding the door for him.

"Angel, why you kill my man?"

"Who?" she asked as if she had done nothing.

"You know who, Qwan."

"Well, I figured that since that nigga turned state he was a threat to us all."

How could he debate that? What she said was true.

"So, the two of you straight?" he asked, staring down at them as he paced the center of the floor. He had heard all about the two of them warring in the streets for territory, and he had heard the story of how Craze found Angel about to kill Roc.

"What's wrong with you, fucking with little kids, man?" Dutch asked her.

"She's crazy," interrupted Roc.

Angel didn't answer. She knew she was wrong, and she knew

if she started that tit-for-tat shit, Dutch would simply shut her down.

"Listen, if we're going to move forward, we got to leave all that bullshit behind us. We have the opportunity to make more money than we ever would have on the streets of Newark pushing drugs on the block."

"How?" Roc asked.

"With these," Dutch said, reaching into his pocket and flashing them a handful of sparkly ice.

"Wow," said Angel, as if hypnotized, reaching out as Dutch poured the contents into her hand.

"That's nothing. They got diamond mines in Africa, and right now I'm in a position to own and control a piece of the diamond trade."

"I don't understand. How'd you get into diamond mines in Africa?" asked Roc. The thought seemed surreal.

Dutch sat down and told his friends everything that had transpired. He told them how Odouwo had approached Craze and helped sneak him out of the country. He told them how he and Craze had put in work for Odouwo in exchange for their freedom. He told them about the assassination of Tita and how Odouwo's family was now in control because of him.

"But you killed Kazami. How could you trust that motherfucker?" Angel questioned.

Dutch explained the connection and how Kazami had intended to kill his father and his uncle. With them out of the way, he was the next heir in line to inherit the throne.

"Who would have ever thought?" said Roc, as he got the picture Dutch defined.

"Yeah, but still, I don't know if I would trust this Odouwo guy," said Angel, knowing what they had done to Kazami.

"I don't trust him. I don't trust him at all. I don't trust any of them. But he kept his word. He paid for your freedom and he helped get you here. But for now he's using me like I'm using him. Don't worry, I have something planned that's gonna fuck him up. He don't even see this shit coming. That's part of the reason I wanted you two to come here with me."

"So what do you want us to do?" Angel inquired.

"For now, nothing, just lay low. When the time comes we're going to strike hard. Odouwo won't even see it coming. By the time he figures out what happened we'll be long gone."

"Is any of this going to involve murder?" Roc asked, wanting to know what he was facing.

"Hopefully not, but you know how shit can get. We just gotta be ready for anything."

Roc knew that probably meant yes, and he was afraid of that. He didn't want to become the vicious, ruthless monster that he once was. But deep down inside he knew it was inevitable.

"I understand you brought your peoples along for the ride?" asked Dutch looking at Angel.

"Yeah, I couldn't leave her behind."

"You couldn't?" he questioned, as if that was clearly the wrong choice of words. "Or you mean you didn't want to?" he asked, knowing the difference.

"Dutch, she saved my life. I'm telling you she's good. Wait till you meet her. You're gonna love her," assured Angel.

"I hope so, 'cause you lost one for that bullshit, ya heard?" he asked, as if he were Hov himself.

"Yo, I almost forgot. I got something to tell you," said Craze, wondering how to break the family news.

"What?" asked Dutch, still ready to fuck with Angel about this broad that apparently had her twisted.

"Umm...well...it's your moms," said Craze, not sure how to tell him.

"What happened?" asked Dutch, all eyes on Craze.

"Nothing, nothing, she good," said Craze, still hesitating.

"Well, what's the problem?"

"She couldn't come 'cause your pops is real sick and she said she had to stay behind to take care of him. She said she couldn't leave him." Craze stopped, saying no more. He figured there was enough for Dutch to digest in that one sentence. And there was.

"My father?" Dutch asked, as if Craze was talking about somebody else's dad.

"Yeah, I seen the nigga, too. You look just like him, just like him."

Dutch got up and walked across the floor. He stared out the window into the Paris night sky. *My father.* The two words kept bouncing in his head. He couldn't believe what Craze had just said. His mother was with his father and they were together. The thought gave him a comfort he had never had, a comfort he knew his mother had yearned for all his life.

"My moms is all right?" he asked, as if that was all that mattered.

"She's good, man. She was real happy to see me and even happier to know that you were all right," added Craze, letting Dutch know Delores was exactly where she wanted to be and she was just fine.

He turned back to his friends, elated at the fact that the gang was all here, ready to ride or die for him, just like old times. Little did he know that the ride was about to get rough, and he would need his friends more than they had ever needed him.

ROC WIT' ME

Nina put her coat on and grabbed her purse. She hurried down the busy street and into a tiny café. Hungry, she asked for a cup of coffee. The gentleman behind the counter passed her the cup.

"A dollar and fifty cents," he said, waiting for her to pay him.

She looked in her wallet, but her money was gone. "Umm... just one minute, please. I'm so sorry, I can't seem to find my money," she said, as a young man slid a dollar and fifty cents onto the counter. She looked up and it was Trick.

"Trick, what are you doing here?" she asked, as if staring at a ghost.

"I'm here to save you," he said, as she dropped the cup of coffee, spilling the black liquid all over herself. Her skin boiled and burned. Nina screamed in agony as she popped up from a deep sleep covered in sweat.

"You all right?" asked Dutch, realizing she had been dreaming.

"I had a dream. It was my brother," she said, rubbing her chest, still sitting up in the bed.

"Lie back down. Go back to sleep," said Dutch, having no sympathy for her dead brother or her dream.

Nina lay back down next to him. As he drifted back to sleep, she lay silently thinking about her brother and what he said to her in her dream. *I'm here to save you.* So much time had passed since he was brutally gunned down in front of their mother's home. Until now, Nina had stayed vigilant against the forces that took his life. She had developed a deep-seated hatred for thugs, guns, crime, drugs, and anything that resembled a fraction of the reason why her brother had been killed. When she first met Dutch, he was that fraction, and that was why she had refused to commit. She refused his love, refused his life, and now here she was, lying next to him.

"Forgive me, brother, forgive me," she whispered.

Roc awoke the next morning with thoughts of his wife and his children. He missed them terribly. He wanted desperately to hear her voice; he wanted her to tell him to come back home. He wanted to hear that she needed him. He paced around his hotel room, trying to decide if he should call. He knew it wasn't wise. He knew her line was tapped, but he couldn't wait any longer. He grabbed his jacket and made his way outside and down the street. He found a phone booth next to a tiny café and decided to make the call.

The phone rang three times before someone picked up.

"Hello," answered a man, the voice familiar to him.

Thrown off guard, he asked for his wife. The man didn't say anything, creating a moment of silence.

"It's Rahman," the man whispered, knowing his name.

"Hello," Ayesha softly said when she got on the phone.

"Yo, what the fuck is going on? You got some nigga in my house?" he growled at her.

"Where are you?" she asked, not having heard from him in a month of Sundays.

"It don't matter where I'm at. Who's that nigga you got in my house?" he asked again, ready to hop a plane and strangle her.

"Brother Faheem," she whispered.

"Faheem? From the Masjid?" Rahman asked, his heart dropping.

Ayesha didn't say anything. She didn't have to. Rahman already knew.

"What is he doing there?" Rahman asked, fire in his eyes.

"Do you really want to go there?" she asked, knowing there was no coming back if they did.

"Ayesha, don't play games with me! I asked you what is he doing there?!" Rahman shouted.

"I married him at the Masjid two days ago. He's my husband," she said, shooting a dagger through his heart.

"What? How could you do this to me? What the fuck is wrong with you?" he yelled, his heart sinking lower and lower with every word she spoke.

"I didn't do anything! You did this to yourself! You did this to us! I begged you not to leave but you did anyway! You knew I needed you and you left me anyway, for what? Huh, Roc, for what? I need someone that wants to be with me, that won't leave me. Faheem loves me and he loves the children. He's here for me when I need him."

"Fuck Faheem! Fuck you, too, Ayesha. You ain't shit, you

hear me? You ain't shit. And when I get back I'm going to kill that motherfucker, you hear me? He's a dead man walking," said Roc, meaning every word he spoke.

Ayesha hung up before Roc could say another word or make another threat. When he called back, she wouldn't answer and simply took the phone off the hook. He tried a few more times, but the line was busy. He hung up the phone and tried for calm in the middle of his fury. He walked back to the hotel, to his room.

Roc was very angry. He remembered that nigga Faheem from the Masjid. He always sat next to him during prayer. His fake ass was merely pretending. Roc never thought that a brother from the Masjid would break the code and bed his wife. *Is this nigga crazy?* For anyone who knew him, to turn against him and move in on his wife and family, they had to know they were wrong. And never in a million years did he think that Ayesha would turn to another man, especially one that he knew. He honestly believed that she would wait for him to return. Roc was so angry all he could think of was killing Faheem, even if it meant going back to prison. He didn't realize his own jealousy. He didn't realize his own anger. Out of nowhere he punched the wall and hurled a clock radio at the television, cracking its screen into a thousand tiny pieces that fell to the floor.

He heard a knock at the door. Slowly he opened it and peeked out.

"You all right in there, motherfucker? I can hear you all the way down the hall," Craze said, standing barefoot, covered only by a pair of Fruit of the Loom boxers.

"Nothing, man, nothing," said Roc, walking away from the door.

"Got to be something—television all fucked up, holes in

the wall and shit," said Craze, observing the scenario as he lit a morning blunt to get the day started.

"It's Ayesha. She's fuckin' with this nigga named Faheem. The mothafucker is at my house right now. He just answered the phone. I'm gonna kill this mothafucker, Craze. I swear to Allah I'm going to kill him. I need to leave here tonight."

"I don't think it's a good idea for you to go home right now," advised Craze, knowing that nigga wasn't going nowhere.

"Yo, I can't let this nigga be around my kids."

"You can't change what is already done. He's already there, she's with him. You said it yourself last night. You guys broke up. So what do you care who she's with? You can only care about yourself and your kids, nothing else."

Roc sat down on the bed and began to rock back and forth, holding his head. The thought of Ayesha and Faheem in bed together made his stomach turn. How could she do that to him, how? He realized at that moment that he had made the right decision by leaving, and that she wasn't for him. She wasn't who he thought she was.

"Yo, Roc, you know I'm here for you, if you want to talk," Craze said, placing his hand on his shoulder, ready to crawl back in bed with his companion from last night.

"I'm good, it's all good. I'm okay, it's okay. You're right, I can't change what's done. I walked away and so did she. It's good, it's all good," said Roc, trying to get a perspective on the situation and keep his composure all at the same time.

"You sure you straight? 'Cause I know you got a lot going on with yourself," said Craze understandingly.

"Naw, nigga, I'm all right," said Roc, embracing his friend and giving him a pound.

" 'Cause shit, I used to know this nigga named One-eyed

Roc. He was my friend and I been looking for him now for a long time," said Craze, waiting for Roc to respond.

"Don't worry, I'm right here, baby. One-eyed Roc is back." Roc smiled.

"That's what's up," said Craze, giving Roc a pound before walking back to his room.

Newark, New Jersey

It was ten o'clock and Delores was fast asleep when she was awakened by the sounds of screams. It was Bernard again, having another nightmare. She went into the bedroom where he was sleeping and held his hand. He was covered with sweat. He screamed out in agony again.

She bent over the bed, rubbing his forehead gently, waking him out of his sleep.

"It's okay, Bernard, I'm here," she said, taking a towel and using it to wipe his face.

He opened his eyes and stared up at her, not saying a word.

"You okay?" she asked as he began to weep like a little boy. "Oh, my God, Bernard, what is it? What happened?" Delores didn't know what to do. She sat quietly on the bed with him, still holding his hand.

"They killed 'em, Delores. They killed them all," he said, shaking as if he was scared to death.

"Who, baby, killed who?" she asked, wanting desperately to help him.

"All of 'em," he said, staring into space somewhere far, far away.

"Bernard, all of who?"

He looked around the room for a moment, silently remembering 1948 and a warm summer evening that would change his life forever.

"I was ten years old. My daddy had come from killing hogs. I remember that night. Momma cooked that pig meat up and made some soup and some homemade bread and we all sat down and was eating when a band of white men covered in white sheets on horses galloped around the front of the house calling for my daddy to come outside. Turned out they believed that the hogs my daddy and his friends had killed earlier that day were stolen from Bob Olsen's hog farm."

Bernard went on to describe in detail how his mother was able to get him and his brother safely out the back window.

"Run into the woods, you hear me, and don't look back." That was the last time his momma would ever speak to him. Just as his body hit the ground, knocking over his little brother, he heard the Ku Klux Klan bust down their door. The screams of his older sister rattled his ears, and he could hear his mother begging for her life. His father fought them off as best he could but was no match for the gang of men. They hogtied him and made him watch as they burned a cross and set his house on fire after savagely raping and beating his wife and daughter to death.

"You fucking niggers think you can steal and get away with it, but you're gonna learn. God sayeth the word, nigger. Thou shalt not steal. God sayeth the word. God sayeth the word. Say it nigger, say it."

"I didn't steal nothing, I didn't. I swear to God I didn't steal no pigs," Rufus Harrison pleaded as the men tied him up and dragged him back into the woods. Rufus was telling the truth. He had traveled all the way to Rosewood and bought the pigs from Wallace Gaines of the Gaines family. No one had stolen anything. It was just pure hatred, pure jealousy, and the American way of treating blacks at that time. Little Bernard and his smaller brother, William, could see the sticks of fire through the woods and could hear their father's screams of torment ringing in the night air. They tiptoed through the woods toward the sounds of their father's screams. They crouched in the shrubs behind a tree and watched as their father's bloody body was stood up, both his arms held tightly, as one of the men walked straight toward him and with a sharp razor sliced off his ear. Rufus yelled in pain, screaming in agony. They quickly lifted him off the ground and onto a horse. The side of his head was bleeding profusely from where his ear had been cut off as a souvenir.

"Daddy," whispered Bernard at the sight of his tortured and barely alive father. They took a noose and placed it over a pleading Rufus's head as he sat on the back of a horse under a tree branch. Seconds later one of the KKK fired a shot in the air, causing the horse to buck, leaving Rufus dangling from the tree branch, the sound of his neck cracking as the noose tightened caused a young William to scream out for his father.

"Daddy!" the tiny boy screamed in pain watching his father swing from the tree branch.

The white-hooded men turned around with their hoods over their faces lifted, and Bernard could see them clearly. He knew all of them. It was Sheriff Faulkner, Deputy Cotton, Mister Boss who was the local shoesmith, Mister Murphy who ran the general store, Mister McMellon who had the local barbershop, and Mister Carroll who worked with Mister Murphy. He even recognized some of the locals: Mister Allen, Mister Brewer, and Mister King, Mister Volpe, Mister Wiese, Mister Koon, Mister Wind, and Mister Powell. There were many more, wearing those white robes and pointy hoods, but young Bernard didn't know them.

"Get them little black bastard niggers," yelled Sheriff Faulkner as he covered his face with his white pointy hood.

"Get 'em! Don't let them get away!"

Bernard remembered that fateful night. He grabbed his little brother's hand and took off like a jackrabbit. Scared of being tortured by the white-hooded men, he ran faster than he had ever run in his life. He never felt his brother's hand break free from his. All he remembered was the pitch-black night, his pounding heart, and being surrounded by fear as he dodged through the trees in the dark, shadowed forest.

"I lost his hand. I lost my brother's hand," said Bernard, staring into Delores's eyes with his own, full of sorrow and pain. "I stopped running and I turned around and I waited for him. I thought he'd be running in back of me, but he never came. So I turned around and went back into the woods. I must've walked ten miles looking for my little brother, and just as the dawn was turning the morning sky gray, I found him…all hung up in a tree," he said, his voice cracking as tears ran down the side of his face.

Delores didn't walk in his shoes, but she understood that his shoes had to have hurt his feet, real bad. She had her own horror stories of being degraded, being denied, and being treated like something secondhand. She didn't doubt one word he spoke.

"A man found me in the woods and took me home. I never saw my family again. He named me James after his family," he said, staring off into the distance. "All my life, I've been fighting…fighting and hating. I hate them for everything they took from me, everything they did to me; to this day, I still do."

Delores didn't say anything. She understood him and she understood his reasoning. He had every right to feel the way he did. His family had been brutalized, tortured, mentally degraded, taught to believe white was better, white was good, white was God, and black was nothing, and therefore he was nothing. As far as Delores was concerned, America had owed a debt to blacks and America needed to ante up. She had raised their son to believe that notion as well.

"It's okay, Bernard, I understand, you know I understand," she said, comforting him. "Everything will be all right, don't you worry. One day, things will be different, one day."

Paris, France

"Are you ready, Nina?" Dutch asked politely, waiting to take Nina's arm.

He had planned an evening in Paris. First they would have dinner at one of Paris's most exclusive restaurants, L'Arpège, then Moulin Rouge. Even though Nina had seen the movie, it couldn't compare to actually sitting in the historic theater. Following the show, Dutch drove out to the countryside. A full moon lit up the night sky as Dutch pulled into a lookout spot on top of a hill.

Nina was speechless looking out at the city lights below.

"I used to come out here and think about you," Dutch said, looking into her eyes. "And you would fill my mind."

"Can I ask you a question?"

"Sure," Dutch replied.

"Why did you wait so long to tell me you were alive? Why did you let me think you were dead all those years?"

"Many reasons. The first was my freedom. I couldn't tell anyone, not even my own mother. The second reason was you refused me once before, remember? All those invites asking you to meet me . . . You never showed," he said, remembering everything like it was yesterday. "I didn't think you were willing to start over again. So, when it was time for Craze to go back for Angel and Roc, I decided to come for you again."

"You did." Nina smiled, thinking of the past three years.

"Yeah, I did," said Dutch seriously.

"Did you think I would come?"

"I knew you would," Dutch replied with confidence.

The two of them sat looking down at the city. It was a perfect date on a perfect night, but little did Dutch know that it wouldn't stay perfect for very long.

LIVE WIRE

The next day, Odouwo phoned Dutch and set up a meeting. He was on his way to Paris, after a short stay in Switzerland, then back to Nigeria. His power was growing, and he was selling more diamonds around the world than DeBeers, all from his own mines. And now with his uncle in place he could have what he wanted—oil. The permits to drill and the licenses to sell and export oil had been restricted and inaccessible until now. With the diamonds and now the possibility of drilling for oil, the Odouwo wealth and riches were endless.

Mr. Odouwo called Dutch to let him know he was downstairs and on his way up to the penthouse suite. Odouwo rolled his large Louis Vuitton suitcase across the expansive lobby floor and took the elevators up. The elevator door opened and Odouwo entered.

"Craze. How are you doing, my friend?"

"I'm well. And you?"

"I'm very good. Today is a very, very good day. It is so wonderful to see you again," Odouwo said, greeting everyone. "Mr. James, may I speak with you in private?"

Dutch gave the signal and Craze waited for the Charlies before closing the door behind him. Mr. Odouwo waited for the door to close before he took a seat at the table.

"So what brings on this sudden visit?" Dutch asked, trying to figure out what he was up to.

"Well, I have great news, great news indeed. A deal is on the table for our Sierra Leone mine. A company called Lancaster, an Australian diamond mine, offered five hundred million dollars today."

"Five hundred million." Dutch smiled as the word million rolled off his tongue.

"I knew this news would please you. I wanted to deliver it to you myself. I figured a toast was appropriate."

Dutch had nothing but gratitude for the man who had helped save his life and had changed his destiny. Mr. Odouwo had brought Dutch to Paris and shown him an entire other world. Dutch had managed to save close to $60 million over the past three years. But now with the cash out of a half billion, Dutch's take would be a cool quarter billion. Not bad for a brother from Newark, New Jersey.

"I just need you to do one thing for me, Dutch." He then reached inside his suit pocket and pulled out some paperwork. "I just need you to sign this agreement between us for the quarter billion dollars, and just for signing," he said, rolling the Louis Vuitton suitcase over to where they sat, "here is an initial payment of twenty million until the deal is finalized." Odouwo watched as Dutch opened the suitcase and looked at the stacked rows of money. Dutch took the Mont Blanc pen Odouwo had laid next to the paperwork and signed his name.

"You will hear from me in the next few days, as soon as everything is finalized," said Odouwo, folding the paperwork back into an envelope.

Dutch shook Mr. Odouwo's hand and walked him to the door. Craze, Angel, and Roc were out in the hallway when Mr. Odouwo came out of the room.

"You all have a good day," Mr. Odouwo said, smiling, as he tipped his head and walked down the hall.

"Everything good?" Craze asked once Mr. Odouwo was out of sight.

"The best it could ever be." Dutch smiled, not letting the cat out of the bag just yet. He wanted to make sure Odouwo came through with the money. And he would. Odouwo had every intention of getting Dutch out of the way, completely.

While Angel was off with her cohorts, Goldilocks snuck out of the hotel and made contact with Director Burns.

"Everything is fine, sir. Just one question. Why is Agent Shipp overseeing my operation, sir?" Kimberly snipped at the director. She had waited for the perfect opportunity to phone in just to ask that question.

"Look, Reese, everyone needs backup in the field. He's there to assist you, not take your case. I know who infiltrated Dutch's organization. You just do your job and let Agent Shipp do his, you got that?" asked the director, not wanting to hear about anyone's personal feelings until Bernard James had been brought to justice.

"Yes, I understand, sir," she said.

"You just do your job and bring down James."

Agent Reese hung up the phone and continued jogging as if nothing had happened. She ran back to the hotel where Angel was waiting for her.

"Where you been?"

"Nowhere, baby, just went for a little exercise," said Kimberly, lying as usual.

"Well, come on, get dressed. We're going out," said Angel, already undressing.

"Okay, where we going?"

"With Dutch, out to dinner," said Angel, unexpectedly.

"Okay, let me hop in the shower." Reese closed the door behind her. *This is it, tonight's the night. I just need to see your face. Please let me see him, please let me see him.*

She dressed hurriedly, then slid on a Citizen watch that Director Burns had given her. It was fully loaded with all kinds of gadgets and intel devices. Angel and Goldilocks exited the elevator and walked through the lobby and out the hotel doors to a Suburban that was parked outside waiting for them. Craze opened the doors and Goldilocks and Angel got inside.

Sitting right there in broad daylight was the man the FBI had been hunting for the past three years.

"Dutch, this is Goldilocks, and that's Nina," said Angel, not realizing she had just sealed their fate. "I think you know everyone else," Angel added, referring to Craze and Roc.

"Hi, nice to meet you," said Goldilocks, extending her hand and shaking Dutch's. *I got your black ass now, motherfucker. You're going down.* Goldilocks smiled and took her seat next to Angel.

Craze got back into the driver's seat and sped down the block. They were going out to celebrate and were dining at La

Chaumière. Once inside, Roc took a quick glance at the menu and had no idea what to order.

"I'll take what you're having. I got to go to the bathroom."

Roc left the table and walked up a flight of stairs to the bathroom.

Just as the waiter walked over to their table to take their order, Craze noticed three unmarked cars speeding into the parking lot.

"Yo, hold the fuck up. You see that?" he asked Dutch, whose instincts had him up from the table, his gun in hand.

"It's the Feds! We gotta get the fuck out of here!" he yelled to alert Angel as he pulled Nina from her seat.

They all looked through the window and saw the men hopping out of the cars. Goldilocks recognized them immediately. She wasn't sure if she should blow her cover and pull out her gun on them or go with the flow and escape alongside Angel.

Before Goldilocks could think twice, Dutch and Nina had busted through the double doors of the kitchen and were making their way out the back of the restaurant.

"Come on. Run, we gotta get outta here, it's the Feds," said Goldilocks, as if she wasn't one of them, grabbing Angel's arm. Angel pulled out her gun and fired four rounds at the agents as they came through the restaurant's front door.

"Hurry," said Goldilocks, running in the direction of Dutch, not wanting to lose him.

Roc hit the bottom of the staircase, saw Angel shooting at the three agents, took out his gun, and popped off in their direction. He caught one of them in the shoulder blade as he dashed across the dining room and through the kitchen's double doors behind Angel. The two of them ran out the back door and hopped into the van behind Goldilocks. Craze sped away as the other two agents busted through the back door of the restaurant.

Roc fired out the van's window, causing them to close the restaurant door and stay inside as they made their getaway.

Nina was completely flustered and bewildered, shaken and teary-eyed. "It's okay. We're okay," said Dutch, trying to comfort her. His mind was working a mile a minute, as was Craze's.

"All this time we been here, we been straight, and now out of the fucking blue the FBI just pop up for dinner?" asked Dutch, shaking his head, knowing something wasn't right.

"Shit don't seem right," added Craze, feeling exactly where his man was taking this shit to. Craze circled the block, then pulled into a parking lot and parked the Suburban.

Dutch hopped out of the van and Craze quickly jumped out behind him. "Everybody, wait right here. I'll be right back," said Craze as he followed Dutch. The two walked to a staircase where Dutch turned and faced Craze.

"You think Roc set us up?" he asked.

"Roc? Why would he do that?"

"I don't know, this nigga shows up and now all of a sudden so do the FBI? I can't believe this shit. I got to get the fuck out of here," said Dutch, peeking at the lot and the Suburban.

"I don't think Roc would do no shit like that."

"What if the phone was tapped when he be trying to call home to Ayesha's dumb ass?"

"Then they would have gotten us in the hotel, right?" asked Craze. "What about this Goldi bitch Angel thinks is so great. I don't like her."

"What she do?"

"Nothing, I just don't like her," said Craze.

Dutch thought about it for a second. "Yo. Where did Angel even meet that bitch at?"

"They met up while Angel was doing that bid."

"Angel gonna have to cut that bitch loose."

"She shouldn't have brought that bitch in the first place."

"Not yet. Let's just watch this bitch for a minute."

"Fuck! We let them get away!" Agent Shipp was up in arms when he realized they had lost their target.

"Agent Reese has activated a tracking device, sir," said Agent Cromwell, looking at a laptop screen. Her tracking device was sequenced with their intel, so they could track her through the computer generated map.

"Come on, we can't afford to lose them now."

Agent Shipp monitored the tracking indicator as Agent Cromwell deciphered their exact location.

"Agent Reese is in that building on the southwest corner, sir," Cromwell advised, pointing to the building across the street.

"You're sure?"

"She's in there, sir. We got her location pinpointed and locked. If she moves, we'll know about it."

"Got 'em," he exclaimed, and a big smile came across his face. He knew that Dutch was a sitting duck who was about to get fucked. Shipp pulled out a phone and called in for backup so that the entire place would be surrounded.

You can run, but you can't hide. I got you now, Dutch. I got you now.

THE GREAT ESCAPE

Dutch had prepared for this day from the moment he had set foot in Paris. If, God forbid, he ever had to be on the run, as he was now, he wanted to have easy access to what he needed to get away. Time was of the essence for him. The faster he got his money, the faster he could dash away and disappear into thin air. His time in Paris had been well spent, well planned, and well thought out. Mr. Odouwo had served the purpose of providing employment, and Mr. Odouwo had given him ample business opportunities, making him wealthy beyond imagination. He had traveled extensively and was accustomed to the finest of everything money could buy. And now he would walk away from the life he had built over the past three years. The fortunate thing was that he could start over.

He had a little more than eighty million saved and was comforted by the knowledge that Nina was there and that she loved him. It was even more of a comfort to him to know that his friends weren't behind bars, locked in cells like caged animals. He had done all that he had to do to get them their freedom. Now, he had to make sure they stayed free. Craze was stuffing the piles and stacks of money into oversized duffel bags. Dutch was loading guns and ammunition into another.

"Grab one of those containers and help me dump this gasoline," Angel told Goldilocks as she began to pour gasoline all over the hardwood floor.

Goldilocks had no choice but to assist. *Where the hell are they at?* She picked up the container and fooled around with the top, wasting time.

"I can't get the cap off," she spat with frustration, as if she couldn't.

"Just grab another one and start upstairs! Come on, hurry up!"

Goldilocks ran up the steps to where Dutch and Craze were. She stepped over broken sheetrock as she walked down the hallway. Dutch had hidden his money between the walls; all $82,327,593 of it. She heard someone coming out of the room and quickly grabbed the container of gasoline and started dousing the floor with it, pretending to be working hard.

"Come on, hurry up, we about to get the fuck out of here," Craze said as he and Dutch rushed by, carrying the duffel bags downstairs. Roc was at the bottom of the stairs taking the bags of money and carrying them out to a van that was parked out front.

Nina just stood watching as everyone moved about the room. The situation was a little more than she had bargained for. Dutch hadn't changed, the only thing that had was his zip code. Nina realized that now that she was inside the belly of the beast. Goldilocks and Angel were about to set the place ablaze, while Dutch, Craze, and Roc got the money and the guns into the van.

"All right, that's it. We're out of here. Let's go," said Craze, passing Roc the last two duffel bags to carry to the van just as FBI agents bum-rushed the perimeter, guns aimed and ready to do what they do.

"FBI! Everybody down on the ground *now*!" one of the agents shouted, waving his rifle at Craze.

Nina dropped down to the floor as Roc dropped the money bags and dove behind a wall for cover as bullets flew from the FBI's automatic weapons. Craze and Angel ducked down, crouching in the living room. Nina crawled behind a chair, her heart pounding in fear. Her mind was scrambling for a safe place to hide.

Goldilocks was on the other side of the room, parallel to Craze and Angel. She ducked and dove for cover as shots continued to ring out behind the wall that concealed Roc. That's when they heard the sound of a helicopter hovering above them. *Damn, we'll never get away with a helicopter following us,* Roc figured to himself, knowing a helicopter would spot them the minute they set foot outside the door. He loaded his automatic weapon. Just as he was about to stick his head around the wall, he saw Nina out of the corner of his eye crawl across the floor on all fours, into a coat closet, where she shut the door safely behind her.

"Cover me," said Craze as Angel began to fire off rounds at the FBI. He ran across the floor to the staircase. An FBI agent was about to fire at him just as Angel shot him down. *That's my girl,* thought Craze as he made it to the top of the staircase and into the room where he had left a shoulder-launched Lau 65-D missile launcher. He loaded the weapon and held it over his left shoulder out the window. He could see the agents scrambling below him as the local law enforcement worked alongside the FBI, surrounding the house. Craze could hear the helicopter's propellers and engine before the chopper came in sight. He fired the missile, the force throwing him back and he leaned against the wall. He watched as the missile flew straight for the helicopter and met its target in midair, causing a thunderous blast and propelling pieces of the burning chopper to the ground. Craze dropped the missile launcher and ran back downstairs.

Roc grabbed a nine-millimeter from the bag and fired at two agents who were closing in on him. Angel had caught a gun in midair that Roc threw to her. She spun around, firing a barrage of bullets, killing three other agents and taking down two more. Nina was inside the closet on the floor in the corner with her knees balled up to her chest, her chin bent, almost touching her knees, and she had her eyes shut tight while she prayed to God that he spare her life. *Please, God, please, don't let me die in here. Please, God, I will do the right thing. I just want to go back home. Please don't let me die.*

Roc, Angel, Dutch, and Craze were strategically targeting the FBI agents and had killed all but the two remaining agents in sight. And just as Roc was about to peel himself from behind a wall and fire at their backs, Goldilocks came from around the wall and fired a single bullet, hitting him in the neck and taking him down. Roc turned as she lowered her weapon, looking around the room, as he fell backward to the ground. As it fell, Dutch could see half of Roc's body from behind the wall. He fired at the remaining two agents in the house and ran over to Roc and knelt beside him.

"Roc," he called out to his friend, as blood gushed from the side of his neck. He bent over his body, taking Roc's hand in his own.

"Go..." Roc said, spitting blood as he tried to speak the name of the bitch who had gunned him down.

"Don't talk," said Angel, figuring Roc was trying to tell them to get away.

Craze ran over to a window and peeked at the police, who were now outside, barricading themselves behind their cars. "They've got the place surrounded," said Craze.

"Goldi..." Roc whispered before his head bent, his eyes closed, and he let out his last breath.

Dutch looked at Angel, who was next to him. Then he turned around, focusing his eyes on Goldilocks. It made sense. It made perfect sense. Dutch knew exactly what Roc was trying to tell him. He looked around the room. There were no doors, no windows where Roc had been standing behind the wall. He was in a safe spot, one of the safest. And Goldilocks had been the only one next to him, and now he lay dead, the police everywhere, and he was trying to say her name. Why hers? To Dutch, it all made sense. As soon as she got there, the FBI did, too. He didn't have time to put it all together, but he knew that was what Roc had been trying to tell him.

"Give up, James! You can't win! You got sixty seconds, James, before we tear-gas the place. Come out now with your hands up. You got nowhere to hide. Give it up. Live to see another day," Agent Shipp shouted into a bullhorn from the front of the house.

Craze fired shots at Agent Shipp, a bullet clipping the bullhorn as Shipp dropped it and ducked for cover behind the door of his car.

"We gotta get out of here," said Craze.

"But how? We're trapped," said Angel, not knowing what Craze did.

Dutch looked at Roc's dead body, madder than a mad hatter about his money and his guns, which were outside in the van. *Fuck!* He was so pissed his blood was boiling.

He raised his P-90 and pointed it at Goldilocks. Angel saw what he was about to do and cried out as Craze turned around.

"What are you do—" Goldilocks asked as Dutch fired one shot, hitting her at point-blank range. For a split second she stood upright as blood drizzled out a tiny hole in her forehead. Her eyes closed and her body slumped to the floor.

"What the fuck! What the fuck you kill her for?" screamed Angel, ready to go toe to toe with him.

"She's the fucking police. She's a fucking cop. I don't know where you got that bitch from, but she's the fucking police," answered Dutch without hesitation. "You heard him, whether you wanted to or not. You fucking heard him just like I did," said Dutch, speaking of Roc's trying to call out her name as he died. Angel stood silent, not really having any options, but knowing deep down the possibilities.

"Where's Nina?" asked Dutch as Craze walked over to the staircase ready to light the trail of gasoline.

"Here I am," she said, standing next to the opened closet door in a state of bewilderment after watching Dutch kill Goldilocks.

He walked over to her, ready to take her hand. "You okay?" he asked, reaching for her.

"Don't touch me," she said as she began to cry. "I just saw what you did. The police are here to arrest you, and before you'll turn yourself in you'll sacrifice the lives of all of us. I can't do this with you, not like this. I want to go home," said Nina, tears in her eyes.

Craze and Angel looked at each other, then at Nina.

"We don't have time for this right now. We have to go—we have to get out of here," said Dutch, again reaching for her hand.

"I can't go with you. I can't do this. I can't live like this. I want to go home, do you understand? I want to go home," she screamed at him, as if it was his fault she was there.

Dutch didn't flinch, he didn't blink, he didn't think twice, and even though he had loved her and wanted nothing more than to have her by his side, she left him with no choice. Before she even knew what happened, she had been shot in the chest, a bullet entering and exiting her body, shooting through her chest like an arrow through a heart. A look of panic and shock was all over her face as her body was thrown against a wall.

She looked at him in disbelief at what he had done to her. She shook her head no at him, her lips parted, and she asked him, "Why?" before taking her last breath.

He turned around and looked at Angel and Craze.

"You guys ready to go?" he asked.

"I need a light," Craze said as he patted down his pockets, not feeling one.

Dutch threw Mrs. Piazza's lighter into the air, the same lighter he had used to light his cigar and signal the courthouse massacre.

"Your lucky lighter." Craze smiled, catching it in midair.

"But how we gonna get out of here?" asked Angel as the first tear-gas bomb crashed through a broken window.

Craze lit the gasoline trail and it quickly blazed up the staircase.

Dutch grabbed Angel's arm as Craze followed the two of them through a door and down a staircase that led to the basement. Dutch had left no stone unturned. The basement had a trapdoor in the floor that would lead them down another flight of stairs and into a three-mile-long drainage tube that they would crawl through. At the end of it they would be right by the river, where Craze had left a small boat. The boat would take them down the river and voilà, another great escape.

SHOT CALLERS,
BIG BALLERS

Nigeria, Africa

Mr. Odouwo stared at the television in total disgust. The breaking news story was featured on every network television station. However, Anderson Cooper was one of his favorite reporters so he always turned his dial to CNN.

"I don't understand! Why did they let him get away?" Mr. Odouwo asked one of his guards, in English. The guard had not a clue what he had just said and no clue how to answer his question. Mr. Odouwo wished that the authorities had done their job and had James in custody by now. Instead, they didn't seem to know if James was dead or alive. Anderson Cooper was standing outside the warehouse in which, the police believed, James was last seen alive. Sixteen FBI agents had lost their lives in the shoot-out and fire at the warehouse and thirty-two more were in critical condition at the local hospital. Mr. Odouwo watched as the bodies of the dead were carried out and lined up in the street outside the warehouse, waiting to be transported to the morgue by ambulance for identification purposes.

"Excuse me, Detective, can you tell us if James's body is among the bodies you've found?" asked a news reporter.

"The bodies have been severely burned, so until we get back the dentals and positive identification reports we can't be sure who any of these bodies are. In the meantime, a manhunt is on, and a million-dollar reward is being posted, just in case James is still out there."

Mr. Odouwo was so disappointed he didn't know what to do. A photo of James flashed across his flat-screen. *Maybe I should up the reward,* he thought to himself, ready to lay out a couple more million dollars for the capture of Dutch. *If only the police and the FBI could do their jobs, I would never have to pay him another dime.* Greed was Mr. Odouwo's only addiction, and for the love of money he would sell Dutch right down the river and count his shares on the way to the bank.

Paris, France

"What the fuck!" Agent Shipp said, looking around after the fire in the warehouse was finally extinguished.

"Sir, we got a body, sir," said an agent, stumbling across Roc's burned and charred body.

Agent Shipp looked around as he saw the bodies of his field agents sprawled among the burned rubble. Nineteen bodies had been pulled from the rubble, and Shipp hoped and prayed that James's body was one of them.

"I can't believe this shit! It's the fucking Essex County Courthouse all over again!" he said as the smell of burned flesh filled his nostrils.

"Agent Shipp, we think we've found the body of Agent Reese, sir," one of the field agents alerted him.

"Where?" he asked, troubled.

"Over here, sir." Agent Shipp looked down at the burned body, recognizing the gold earrings she wore—a flash of the last time they argued in the alleyway reminded him.

"Yeah, that's her all right," he said, bending his head down solemnly before walking back outside. He knew what her loss meant to the department and the investigation. It had taken years to get her inside and now the investigation was over and Agent Reese was dead. Without her, they had nothing. They had no more leads. Agent Shipp sat on the curb, his elbows on his knees and his head bent low. He could hear the director's voice bellowing in his head. Deep down he knew the entire operation was blown now that Reese was dead.

"Don't look so sad, Shipp. You never know, he might just be here in one of these body bags," said another agent, knowing that the possibility of Bernard James being in a body bag were very slim.

"Yeah, maybe, you never know," said Shipp, deep down knowing all too well that James had once again slipped through the cracks.

London, England

Within twenty-four hours, Craze, Dutch, and Angel checked into the Bryanston Court Hotel in downtown London. They had gotten from Paris to London by boat, hitching a ride on a large barge that was transporting Baqri barrels of oil. Dutch knew the Baqris from Tanzania, and once he found out who owned the barge, a phone call was placed and Dutch was snuck aboard. Dutch hadn't spoken more than five words since they escaped from the warehouse. The loss of eighty-three million dollars was more than he could fathom; it gave him a feeling of helplessness. The raid at the warehouse had left him penniless, which made him vulnerable. He could have taken that eighty-three million and gotten away and had a wonderful rest of his life on some glorious island in the middle of nowhere. Now, he was back to ground zero, back to where he started. He knew the only person who could save him was Mr. Odouwo. Odouwo still owed him the $230 million, which he had signed for, and now Dutch needed Mr. Odouwo to advance him something so he could lie low. Little did he know that Mr. Odouwo had no plans of paying him anything.

Dutch picked up the phone and placed an international call to Nigeria, calling Mr. Odouwo directly. He didn't answer, so Dutch called his personal cell phone line.

"Dutch, are you all right? Are you safe?" asked Mr. Odouwo, who answered the call, showing much concern.

"Yes, I'm safe," answered Dutch. He listened to Mr. Odouwo tell him everything that was transpiring on the news. The men spoke freely, and finally Mr. Odouwo asked Dutch what he needed.

"Actually, I need the rest of that money," said Dutch, waiting for a response regarding the $230 million Mr. Odouwo still owed him.

"Well, of course, I understand. How should we do this?" asked Odouwo, ready to set a trap and catch the mouse himself.

"Can you meet me in London?" asked Dutch.

"England?" responded Mr. Odouwo.

"Yeah, there's a hotel in downtown London called the Bryanston Court Hotel."

"Yes, I know the hotel. I can meet you there in two days. Okay, my friend?" Mr. Odouwo asked in all seriousness, as if he'd really be there with a suitcase full of Dutch's money.

"Sounds good to me, Mr. Odouwo," Dutch said, feeling as if a heavy weight had just been lifted off his shoulders. "Two days sounds real good."

Dutch hung up the phone feeling as if all wasn't lost. As long as Mr. Odouwo showed up with the money he owed him in two days, Dutch knew he'd be all right.

Mr. Odouwo hung up the phone and smiled as he stuck his pointer finger in his spirit and stirred the alcohol and Coke. *Poor, poor, Dutch, his time is slowly running out.* And now that Dutch was on top of the world's most wanted list, catching him would require almost no effort.

Paris, France

"Her name is Nina Martin. She was a bank manager living in Newark, New Jersey. No spouse, no kids, no known living relatives," one of the field agents told Agent Shipp as they looked at photos of Nina's body.

"Turns out she was James's girlfriend," said the agent, opening a manila folder and laying several photos on the table for everyone to see.

"We got photos that were taken from the Charles de Gaulle Airport just a few days ago. She was seen here with James's asso-

ciates and Agent Reese," said the agent, pointing to the photo
of Kimberly.

"Why would he bring her all the way over here to kill her?"
asked one of the other agents.

"Who the fuck knows? What I do know is that this motherfucker is borderline psychos-are-us and it's time we take him
down."

It turned out that Shipp's intuition had served him well, and
James's body had not been among the bodies pulled from the
warehouse.

"He could be anywhere in the world by now," said an agent.

"It's like looking for a needle in a haystack," added another.

"I don't care where he is. He can run, but he can't hide. I will
find him; I will bring him down. If I have to go halfway around
the world and back, I will. I'll do whatever it's gonna fucking
take to bring that cocksucker down, do you understand me? I
won't stop until Bernard James is behind bars or until I got his
corpse on a gurney, you got it? And I will bring him down, if
it's the last thing I do!"

Newark, New Jersey

Delores was scooping coffee into her Mr. Coffee filter to brew a
morning cup of joe. She turned on the television in the kitchen
as Bob Barker was waiting for a contestant to spin the wheel
to see if she would win a brand-new car. Bernard was resting
still, doped up on morphine provided by the hospice nurse
who was visiting every morning and every night to check on
his progress.

"Crossing over takes its toll on us all. Are you sure you don't want me to have an ambulance come take him to the hospital?"

Delores declined although she had the opportunity to free herself from the responsibility of caring for a dying man. Actually, she welcomed the burden. It was her pleasure to serve him, even more so in this capacity. All her life she had waited for the man who held her heart. Sure, she had her questions and wanted answers to her whys, but just having him here with her again was enough. Just to know that he had never stopped loving her and that he didn't forget her made it all worthwhile.

She could hear him in the bedroom and made her way to his side. He could barely sip from a straw, barely speak, and of course was barely able to move anymore. The nurse from hospice seemed to feel that he would pass on within the next twenty-four to forty-eight hours.

"Bernard, I'm right here," she said, touching his hand so he could feel comforted. He slowly pulled his hand away from her as he gently began to pull at the shirt he was wearing.

"What? You a little warm?" she said as she helped him pull the shirt over his head, not knowing that some like the exit like the entrance: naked.

His bare-boned chest rose and fell as Delores patted his head with a refrigerated moist towel.

"I'm right here, Bernard. I'm with you, okay? You're not alone, baby. You're not alone."

She was determined she would be there for him and determined that he would not pass over by himself. He had spent his entire life alone, but he wouldn't die that way. That's why she refused let the nurse take him, because she wanted to be there with him until he made his final crossing over. She felt that it was the least that she could do for the man she had loved all her life, the least.

London, England

Dutch was waiting for Mr. Odouwo along with Craze, Angel, and several accompanying Charlies.

Unknown to Dutch, Mr. Odouwo was right downstairs on the third floor in a room preparing himself.

"Are you sure you want to do this?" asked Agent Shipp.

"Yes, of course," said Mr. Odouwo, face to face with the FBI agents who would ultimately pay him the million-dollar reward for Dutch's head.

The agents wired a writing pen and placed it gently in the shirt pocket on Mr. Odouwo's chest. They did a microphone check, and the field agent sitting at a desk next to a laptop transmitter and wearing headphones looked up with his thumb in the air to let them know the device was working properly.

Mr. Odouwo picked the briefcase filled with marked money up off the floor.

"Don't forget: I want James alive. And if he gets away this time, the briefcase has a tracking device and the money is marked, so we'll find him. No matter where he goes, we'll be able to track him down," said Agent Shipp convincingly.

Mr. Odouwo nodded as an FBI agent opened the door for him.

"Don't worry, once you make contact with James and you're safely out of that room, we'll be going in right behind you. He won't get away this time. He's got no place to run and no place to hide," smiled Agent Shipp.

"The entire hotel is surrounded. In a few minutes this will all be over and James will either be dead or be in custody on his way to a lovely nine-by-nine prison cell on Guantánamo Bay." Shipp smiled, thinking of the accolades he would receive for bringing down one of America's most wanted murderers.

Mr. Odouwo and his security team made their way to the elevators and up one flight to the fourth floor. Mr. Odouwo knocked on Dutch's hotel door. Craze carefully peeked out the door before opening it.

"How are you, Craze? It's been such a long time," said Mr. Odouwo, thinking back to the day he phoned Craze and they plotted Dutch's escape from the Essex County Courthouse.

"I'm good, sir, and you?" asked Craze, closing the door behind him.

"Well, my knee has been bothering me a bit. But I must tell you, perfect health is truly a blessing," he said, all smiles, thinking of the quarter billion he would be keeping to himself.

Craze walked out of the room as the two men sat across from each other. Mr. Odouwo opened the briefcase, assuring Dutch that one hundred million was inside it, and giving him an assurance that should he need more money in the future, all he had to do was call.

"Where will you go?" asked Odouwo, just in case he got away.

"An island where no one will ever find me." He smiled, knowing exactly where he was going from here.

"I can have a DHC-6 Twin Otter waiting for you where the *Lucky Stripe* is docked."

"Yeah, that would be perfect, just in case," said Dutch, already knowing how he planned to make it out of the city. But a plan B couldn't hurt right about now.

"I owe you my life, Dutch," said Odouwo, fooling him but good.

"No, I think I probably owe you mine. What you have done for me is beyond the imagination," said Dutch, having no idea at all that the police were right outside the door waiting for Mr. Odouwo to exit safely before barging in.

The two men sat and talked shop for a while. They had a lot of history between them. Actually, they had made a fortune together in the diamond business. Dutch had put in all the dirty work, having bloodstains on his hands. However, the price for what he had done was certainly worth it. The men rose from their seats and Dutch closed the briefcase in front of him.

"Travel well, my friend." Odouwo smiled, shaking Dutch's hand.

"Thank you, thank you for everything," said Dutch, taking the man's hand in his and shaking it.

"I will see you again real soon," said Odouwo. "A hundred million dollars won't last long," he said jokingly, thinking of the government's marked money inside the briefcase.

"Tell me about it," said Dutch, agreeing that one hundred million dollars really wasn't a lot of money at all. And for him, it wasn't.

He let Mr. Odouwo's hand go and the two men embraced.

"In another time," said Odouwo, kissing Dutch's cheek farewell with a kiss of death.

"Another time," said Dutch, knowing that the men would meet again one day.

Mr. Odouwo walked out the door and Craze closed it behind him. Less than thirty seconds later, as Dutch was about to open the briefcase to look at the money inside, the door to the hotel room burst open and field agents stormed in.

"This is the FBI! You are under arrest! Get down now with your hands behind your head!"

Dutch grabbed the briefcase before reaching for his nine-millimeter. Craze was always ready and fired first, behind him Angel and the other Charlies dodged a barrage of bullets as they fired their weapons, dropping FBI agents like flies. Craze busted a window in the bedroom as one of the Charlies made a rope out of sheets for them to scale down the wall. Dutch landed safely on the ground first, behind him Angel, then Craze, along with two Charlies, as the other two Charlies faced off with the FBI in the hotel room. Dutch was still holding the briefcase when snipers on top of a building across the street spotted them and began firing.

"Come on, let's go," said Dutch. He took off and ran across the parking lot to a BMW. Craze used the key to unlock the doors. The three of them hopped into the car—Craze taking the driver's seat while Dutch hopped into the passenger seat and Angel in the back—while the other two Charlies stopped to handle the snipers on the roof before squeezing into the back of the car with Angel.

Out of nowhere a bullet crashed through the glass and pierced Craze's chest, lodging itself between bone and tissue mass. Dutch floored the gas and ran straight through a police barricade as bullets took out the windshield. Craze was bleeding everywhere but still sitting in the driver's seat, Dutch's body literally on top of him as he made the getaway.

"You fucking pieces-of-shit ass cops! I fucking hate you," screamed Angel, grabbing an AK-47 off the car's floor and firing a trail of bullets at the line of police cars following behind them.

"Take out their tires," yelled Dutch as he used his driving

skills from back in the day when he used to steal cars for a living.

Craze could feel his chest cavity and the open wound, the bullet that had pierced him, and he knew he wouldn't make it. That's when he made a decision, as if Buster had told him to, that he hoped would work for the sake of his team.

"I need you to pull over," said Craze.

"I can't right now, I got to lose these guys first," said Dutch, as if, if that was what Craze wanted, then that was what would be done. "You just hang on, you hear me?" he said, wiping a tear from his face.

Angel continued to fire at the oncoming police cars, popping tires, shooting at the drivers, causing them to run into other squad cars, crash, and flip over on their sides. The rapid spray of bullets from the AK-47 was more than the officers in the police cars behind them could handle. With more squad cars approaching from behind, Dutch sped through the congested city.

Agent Shipp and his fellow field agents had now joined the chase and were a few squad cars behind. The Charlies threw grenades out the windows and watched the police cars blow up as they detonated.

"Nice," purred one of the Charlies, slapping a high five with the other.

Even parked cars on the street caught fire from the grenade blasts.

Agent Shipp was speeding at an even ninety-five miles per hour when the police car in front of him ran over an exploding grenade. Agent Shipp swerved to avoid crashing as the car fell out of the sky and flipped on its side.

"Hold on!" yelled Shipp, losing control of the car and smashing into a commercial service vehicle blocking his path. He was unable to drive the car any farther. He looked at his passengers, who were banged up a bit, but all in one piece.

"You guys all right?" he asked as he got out of the car, a little shaken, and watched the car Dutch was helping to operate make the perfect getaway, once again.

"Fuck, not again! He's getting the fuck away!" yelled Agent Shipp. "Come on, men! We can't just stand here! We have to catch that car!" He ran down the street, flagging down another police car.

Somehow Dutch was able to steer a path that left the police in a trail of smoke behind him. Dutch turned down a little side street that led to a narrow alleyway. "We're stopped, Craze," he informed Craze, who was keeping himself as still as possible. "What you want me to do?" asked Dutch, prepared to do anything for his main man.

"Go on, get out of here," he said, staring his best friend in the eyes. "You got to go on without me," said Craze.

"No, that's out of the question," said Dutch, refusing to leave him behind. He was about to throw the car into drive and keep it moving. "I'm not fucking leaving you. You go down, I go down. We all go down together, you dig?" he asked Craze, staring into his eyes to see if Craze understood him loud and clear.

"No, I want you to get out of the car now while you got a chance. I'm not gonna make it, Dutch. I'm not. Please let me hold it down while you guys get away," he said, nodding at him. "Trust me, son, I'll buy you as much time as I can."

Dutch had never imagined shit going down like this. Angel let out a loud scream. "No, this can't be happening!"

Everyone realized at that moment that Craze was going to

sacrifice himself for them. "I love you, Craze," she said, holding his head, kissing the side of his face. "I love you, nigga, for life."

"I love you, too, Angel." Craze smiled, pleased that she was following his order. Standing on the side of the road she looked at the two brothers from different mothers inside the car.

"What the fuck you still sitting there for?" asked Craze, with nothing but love in his voice.

"How the fuck I'm supposed to walk away from you?" asked Dutch, ready to die with him.

"'Cause, nigga, I'ma be all right. I'll be waiting for you on the other side," he said, his eyes pleading for Dutch to go while he had a chance. Dutch watched as blood gushed from Craze's mouth.

"Shit, I'm all fucked up." Craze smiled, sucking in deep breaths of air. "Go on, man." He stopped for a moment and looked Dutch square in the eyes. "I'll meet you at the crossroads, ya heard."

Angel placed two machine guns in the car next to Craze, all the while crying uncontrollably.

"Hurry up and get out of here," Craze commanded, as Dutch closed the passenger car door behind him.

Dutch looked at Craze and a tear rolled from his eye. Craze smiled at his man, knowing Dutch loved him just as much as he loved Dutch. He saw Dutch heave a heavy sigh.

Am I my brother's keeper? Craze thought as he put the car in drive and sped down the street, leaving Angel barely able to stand as she broke down crying in the arms of one of the Charlies.

Craze floored the gas, turned onto a main street, and followed the sounds of the roaring sirens until the police were back on his tail. He drove the BMW through the city streets at over

110 mph, making a right-hand turn, which turned out to be a wrong turn, as he had a brigade of police cars headed straight for him. He tried to elude them and hopped the curb in hopes of getting away. He flew down the sidewalk, crashing into poles and a fire hydrant. People tried to hurry out of the way as Craze mowed them down like bowling pins. "Sorry," he said as he hit a group of elderly people, thinking of Slick Rick. Their twisted bodies flew off the hood and roof of his car and into the air. More police cars joined the chase, coming from side streets, as Craze continued to dip past them all making his way onto the Tower Bridge, which proved to be the wrong move. The other side of the bridge was blocked off by tanks and British soldiers.

"Aiight then, this is how this shit is gonna end," Craze said, slamming his foot on the brakes. *Am I my brother's keeper?* He thought about the proverb and knew what had to be done. He looked into the rearview mirror at the police cars stopped several thousand feet behind him, and he looked across the bridge at the tanks and police cars waiting for him on the side. He had nowhere to go. He sat in the car and he thought through his life. He saw Dutch as a little boy slapping fives with him; he saw everything they had been through, the women, the money, the life he had lived, the sex, the drugs, the hundred-million-dollar monopoly he had helped build, all his happy, all his sad, his moments twisting out broads, and how sad Dutch looked as he saw a tear roll down his face. *I don't think I ever seen that nigga cry. Don't worry, son, it's all good. I got you, my nigga, I got you.* With all his strength he flung open the car door.

"Step out of the vehicle with your hands behind your head," said a voice from a police bullhorn. "You are completely surrounded. Step out of the vehicle with your hands behind your head."

Craze did just what he was told to, pretending to surrender. Bleeding profusely from his chest wounds, he stumbled out of the car, holding his hands in the air. The ledge of the bridge was only six feet away—a hop, a skip, a jump, and a leap away. He thought about what he was about to do and the question popped into his head once more: *Am I my brother's keeper?*

"Yes, I am."

The police stood down as they watched Craze leap off the ledge of the Tower Bridge, his body seemingly suspended in slow motion as it filtered through the air and crashed into the River Thames.

Agent Shipp and his agents had just made it to the scene. Shipp jumped out of his patrol car and watched Craze's body drop, splashing into the river below.

"Where are the others?" Agent Shipp asked the commander in charge.

"It's only him."

"What do you mean—Dutch got away? He got away, again?" Shipp fumed as he called for the FBI air team to patrol the area in their helicopters. But they wouldn't find him. They were too late, and once again Dutch had gotten away without a trace.

THE FINAL FINALE

Newark, New Jersey

Everyone from all over the world watched the devastating news on television and couldn't believe what had happened. An amateur video taken from a cell phone captured Craze's free fall from the top of the bridge. Every news station continued to replay the graphic events, which seemed to come straight out of a Hollywood movie. The FBI didn't relish the thought of Dutch getting away again. They had all the airports and all exit points of the city shut down, leaving no stone unturned. Wherever he was, he wouldn't get far, that was for sure.

Delores Murphy watched the television screen as Craze's body hit the water. She knew that the FBI was closing in on them if Craze was leaping off a bridge to his death. She wondered if Dutch was okay or if he had been injured. A tear dropped from her eye as she watched Craze's body hit the water once again as she flipped through the channels.

"God be with him," said Delores, wishing for just one more moment with her son.

"He is."

Delores turned around at the sound of Bernard's voice. He hadn't spoken in over a week and just as clear as day, she heard him say, "He is." And he said it as if she had nothing to worry about, as if everything was just fine. She looked at him and at the smile that had spread across his face.

"What did you say?" she asked, even though she had heard him. She just wanted to hear him speak again. Then she realized, as she moved closer to him, that even though his eyes were staring straight through her and the smile on his face was big enough to light up Times Square, he was gone. He had passed just like that, just that quickly and taken his last breath with his last words.

"Bernard," she whispered at the sight of his dead body. "Oh, God, no, Bernard...Bernard...Bernard," she said. She kissed the side of his face, then used two fingers to close his eyes. "Now you are free, now you will have your peace, and you won't suffer here or be in no more pain. God rest his soul," she said, before reciting the Lord's Prayer while holding his hand.

"Our Father who art in heaven, hallowed be thy name, thy kingdom come, thy will be done on earth as it is in heaven, give us this day our daily bread, as we forgive those who trespass against us, and lead us not into temptation but deliver us from evil, for thine is the kingdom, and the power, and the glory, forever, amen."

She looked down at the man she had wished for all her life, and the funny thing was she didn't have one tear, not any sadness, only a feeling of enlightenment and gratification. "Thank you, Bernard. Thank you for coming back for me," she said, kissing the back of his hand before gently lifting herself off the bed to call the authorities.

London, England

Dutch, Angel, and the two Charlies ran down the street and around the corner where a parked car was sitting.

"Keep a watch," Dutch said, up to his old childhood ways again as he jump-started the tiny Volkswagen. They all hopped into the car and Dutch drove the vehicle through the streets of London. He had been moving through London for quite some time, shopping frequently at Harrods, dipping in and out of Brussels, but living in Paris. He quickly switched to the only option he had left, which was plan B. He drove straight to the dock, taking less than ten minutes to reach it. He remembered what Mr. Odouwo had said to him the last time they were together. He couldn't believe it, but once again, Mr. Odouwo would be saving his life.

"Whose gonna fly the plane?" asked Angel, confused.

"I can handle it," Dutch said, not knowing if he could or couldn't, but he was willing to die trying if it meant he'd get away. They all ran down the pier to where the plane was parked in the water. An old man, dressed in smelly old fisherman's overalls, green water boots up to his knees, and a cap on his head, was all alone in the middle of the pier fishing. He looked their way and locked eyes with Dutch in disgust.

"You're gonna scare the fish!" he snapped.

"Fuck the fish," Dutch said, running by the bearded old man to the end of the pier, until he reached the yellow plane, parked all by itself.

He held the door, waiting for Angel and the two Charlies to safely board. Then he climbed inside.

"Do you believe we're really gonna do this shit?" said Angel as everyone snapped on their seat belts. Dutch looked around the plane. The console was unfamiliar to him, but he knew the basics.

"I believe we are," agreed Dutch as he switched the engine on, pressed the propeller button, unlocked the gears, and backed out of the dock.

"We are out of here, baby," she screamed, slapping high fives with Dutch and the two Charlies in the backseat.

"Hell, yeah!" one of the Charlies screamed as Dutch pulled back on the throttle, testing it calmly as he sped across the water. He pulled down on the gears as the plane lifted like magic into the air.

"We are flying the fuck out of here. Fucking cops, you can't catch us," Angel screamed. "Yeah, baby!"

While Angel was ranting and raving, slapping high fives with her girls, Dutch looked down at the pier. He could see the fisherman, who was now standing at the edge of the pier, staring up into the sky at them in the plane. He was holding a black box with a long antenna. He took off his cap and waved at Dutch, whose face he could see through the plane's window.

What the fuck? Dutch questioned as their running down the pier replayed in his mind.

He could hear the man's voice as it echoed through his head, "You're gonna scare the fish." The voice behind that face and the voice behind the smelly fisherman's overalls was very familiar. And right before Mr. Odouwo pressed the red button on the detonator to seal Dutch's fate, Dutch recognized him. *Odouwo? What the fuck is he doing out there?* And then it hit him. Mr. Odouwo had set him up. The detonator was a trigger for liquid explosives that were lined throughout the plane. Just as the plane reached twenty thousand feet, Odouwo let the red button go.

Before Dutch could think or speak, the liquid explosives created a ball of fire within the aircraft. The old man standing on the pier could see the heavy flames coming from inside the plane before it exploded and disintegrated in the sky, pieces of the aircraft falling into the water below.

His work was done. He turned around, pushed the antenna back into the detonator, pulled off his mustache-and-beard disguise, and looked at his watch. It was time for cocktails. Mr. Odouwo smiled as he walked back down the pier. *Some things in life a man just has to do himself,* he thought, as a smile spread across his face.

Three Weeks Later

Terrence stood at the grave of FBI Agent Kimberly Reese. He missed her very much. He had never thought of life without her. He had visited her grave every weekend since the funeral. The death of Kimberly shook him in his pants, and he realized how important life really was. He sat a picture of her in a Tiffany frame on his dresser, so she'd know he wouldn't ever forget her.

"You were always worried that you'd go away somewhere and come back and things would be changed...that... somehow, I'd forget you that fast and move on, like you wouldn't have a home to come home to. I just want you to know, you'll always have a home with me, Kim. I'll always be here, okay?

I'll be back to visit you and any time you want to come home, the door's open."

Terrence wiped his eyes and turned from her grave, after placing a beautiful bouquet of flowers at her headstone.

Ayesha signed for the body of her children's father, Rahman, alongside Faheem. They had turned his services over to the Masjid. Ayesha knew that the sisters in the Janazah committee would take care of him.

"Don't worry, sister, we're gonna wrap up brother Rahman real good, Alhamdulillah!" And they did, and Ayesha laid her children's father to rest.

Angel's body was found two weeks later and was transported back to Newark, New Jersey. Her body was so decayed from being in the water so long that she had to be identified by dental records. The relationship with her mother had never been strong, and unfortunately no one had any money to bury Angel. She was cremated by her great-aunt who kept her ashes in the dining-room china cabinet drawer.

The bodies of the two Charlies were also recovered, still strapped into the plane seats. They were sent back to the United States to their families.

One week after burying Bernard James, Sr., Dutch's father, Delores Murphy signed for the bodies, or what was left of the bodies, of Dutch and Craze. She held a memorial to celebrate their lives. People from all over the world came to pay their last respects. The newspapers said that there were over five thousand mourners who attended the memorial services for Dutch and Craze. The police had to be called to shut down streets, direct traffic, and keep order. The following morning, Delores buried the bodies of Christopher Shaw, aka Craze, and Bernard James, Jr., aka Dutch, side by side, as brothers should be.

READING GROUP GUIDE
Discussion Questions

1. Do you wish that Dutch had gotten away?

2. Did you think that Mr. Odouwo was setting him up from the beginning?

3. Did you think that Dutch should have killed Nina or let her go back home?

4. Should Craze have turned himself in or sacrificed his life for Dutch?

5. Do you think Delores did the right thing taking Bernard James, Sr., home with her?

6. Should she have left him behind, as he did her?

7. Should Ayesha have stood by her man, Roc, or taken another husband?

8. Why do you think Angel didn't see through Goldilocks?

9. Do you think that Goldilocks loved her boyfriend, even though she was in another relationship with Angel?

10. Were you satisfied with the ending or do you wish Dutch was still alive?

ACKNOWLEDGMENTS

I would like to thank my family, Mom, Carol, Chucky, Dexter, Brenda, Carl, my children, Jessica, Lucas, and Brandon.

I would like to thank everybody that is in my life, not just today, but those who have been there from the beginning.

I would like to thank my friend Kashan Robinson. You are a good friend, even when you holler at me. You always rep me to the fullest, BK. You always got my back, and I know that you love me. Please know I love you too.

I would like to thank Branson Belchie, for the chronic nigga, and for always having me covered. You are like an old, dusty, blue blanket. You are comfort. A new blanket wouldn't work for me. Thank you for believing in me, thank you for holding me down. Thank you for the way you stand there and watch me fall out and have a mental breakdown, and thank you for helping me get back up. And thank you for that lovely gift, that photo of God knows who that you went all out your way to get for me. Oh my God, I'm rolling on the floor, right now. Yo, B, you be killing me over here, I swear.

I would like to thank Manny Haley because despite the

turmoil you put me through and despite our disagreeing with one another and despite the bullshit, I do believe in you. You always come through for me and I do appreciate having you in my corner. I love you, BK, remember that. We have much to do, let's go!

I want to thank Leon Blue, boy oh boy. If these people only knew what you be doing for me, and if they only knew that you be saving my ass. And to everybody that does know, I got Blue's ass back! I will always be here for you. Thank you again.

I would like to thank Alonzo Harris aka Uncle Boonie. You are a wonderful friend and a good man. Thank you for being my friend.

I want to thank Mia X. First of all, people should know that you have been in my life for the past ten years. And in those ten years, I have told you my life story, and you have told me yours. Thank you for being a long-distance ear and a shoulder for me to cry on. And to think, we've never met and I want you to know I'll probably cry when we do. I love you, thank you for being there, thank you for listening, thank you for understanding me.

I want to thank all the business associates who continually protect my company, all the agents, lawyers, accountants, and consultants that I have the pleasure of working with on a daily basis. Thank you for your expert advice and continued dedication to me and my brand.

I want to thank everyone out there who has read my books and everyone out there who has supported me. I started out the trunk of the car and, to this day, I still am. To all the people who write to me looking for my books and to all those who visit www.teriwoodspublishing.com and purchase my books from me at my Web site, thank you, thank you, thank you, because that is our future and no one can stop what I want to do online and no one can stop you online. As an independent publisher I just want you to really understand the dynamics of what you have done as a consumer and what you have done for me as an author and independent publisher. I thank you from the bottom, and I will see you at www.teriwoodspublishing.com.

And last, I want to thank everybody out there who looks out for me, makes my life pleasurable, and shares life with me. I thank you for being in my corner and I couldn't do life without you.

Don't miss the page-turning second installment in Teri Woods's new series!

Please see the facing page for a preview of *Alibi II*.

Available in 2012

1986

BAMBOOZLED

The State of Pennsylvania v. Bernard Guess
Day One

Nard used all of his willpower to contain himself as he sat, pensive and breathless, while the inside walls of the courtroom seemed to spin uncontrollably. His mind was racing a thousand miles a minute, and he saw his life flash in front of him. *No way. This isn't happening. What is she doing? I'll go to jail for the rest of my life.* It was all he could think as he locked his eyes on the witness, Daisy Mae Fothergill. She was sitting calmly on the stand, nodding ever so slightly as she leaned in to the microphone and gave answer after answer.

"Ms. Fothergill, you say today that you never saw my client, Bernard Guess, before, is that correct?"

"Yes."

"However, this is your signature—is that correct?" Bobby DeSimone asked after walking swiftly to the defense table and picking up an investigative report.

"Yes," Daisy Mae calmly responded.

"Your Honor, I would like this to be marked as Exhibit A," he said, handing the document over to the judge. He turned back to Daisy Mae. "In this document you state that the defendant was with you on the night in question, is that correct?"

"Yes."

"So, now you've changed your mind and you want us to believe that you were lying then?" He arched his eyebrows and stared intently at her. Then he turned and purposely faced the jury while still waiting for her answer.

"I was paid to say what I said."

"So you can be bought. Is that your answer, Ms. Fothergill?"

"Objection, Your Honor. Completely inappropriate," said the district attorney, quickly standing up.

"Sustained. Watch it, counsel!" said Judge Means.

"Just one more question, Your Honor." DeSimone cleared his throat and picked up where he had just left off. "Why should we believe you now?"

"I've told the truth here today."

"Are you sure no one paid you, Ms. Fothergill?"

"Objection, Your Honor."

"Sustained."

"No more questions, Your Honor," said DeSimone, strolling over to his table and seating himself next to Nard.

Even with DeSimone's tricky and clever line of questioning, Nard's heart continued to sink, along with his fate, as he bent his head down and stared into his lap. *She didn't do it. She didn't give me the alibi.* He pondered choking the daylights out of her. *I thought she had me covered. Sticks said she had me covered. What the fuck am I going to do now?*

"Will you be cross-examining, Mr. Zone?"

"Yes, thank you, Your Honor."

The district attorney walked toward the witness stand. "Ms. Fothergill, you said that you were paid to make the statements you formerly made to the private investigator hired on behalf of the defendant, correct?"

"Yes."

"Did anyone bribe you or pay you today?"

"No."

"The statements that you have made today, you've made of your own free will?"

"Yes, that is correct."

"Are you absolutely positive the defendant was not with you on the night in question?"

"I'm positive. He was not with me on the night in question."

"No more questions, Your Honor."

"You may step down, Ms. Fothergill," the judge instructed.

She glanced at Nard's face as she left the witness stand. *God, he looks so mad*, she thought as she was escorted out of the courtroom.

Inside, Nard could be heard screaming at the top of his lungs. "That's it?! She just gets to leave?"

DeSimone looked over at the jury. Their expressions said a thousand words. Daisy Mae Fothergill just shot a missile into his battleship, and now, thanks to his client's outburst, it was sinking.

Four rows behind Nard, a family was rejoicing and a girl's voice could be heard.

"That's what you get! That's just what you get for killing my brother! You know you was up in that house and you the one that killed him!" she shouted, now standing on her feet, ready to jump over the benches and pounce on Nard for the death of her brother Jeremy Tyler.

"Who the fuck is you talking to?" Nard barked at the girl, ready to jump back at her, her family, and anybody else who had something slick to say.

"Order!" Judge Means called out and banged his gavel on its wooden plate.

"I'm talking to you. You know you killed my brother," the girl screamed, tears streaming down her face. Her mother, sister, and two brothers held her back. The oldest brother, Wink, put his arms around her, holding her firmly to his side.

"Be easy, Leslee. You whylin', man. Relax. I'm gonna get the boy, him and his whole fucking family," said Wink, as he smiled at his sister.

"I don't need any more attention drawn to this courtroom." The judge continued banging his gavel. The entire case was already a fiasco in the media; every day camera crews and news reporters were looking for a new angle on the story to headline the nightly news. "Young lady, do I need to have you removed from this court?"

"Naw, we sorry, Your Honor," said Wink. "She good. She not gonna say nothing else."

"Any more disruptions made in this court by anyone, and you will be removed." Then the judge looked at the jury. "You are to disregard the outbursts and opinions made by third parties in this court, and the outburst of the defendant as well."

"I can't believe this bitch just hung me," Nard whispered to DeSimone as the judge continued to direct the jury.

"Nard, calm down. You don't want to do this—not here, not now."

"She just hung me!" Nard hissed.

"Look at me," DeSimone ordered. "I said, not here, not now.

You got that, kid? Not now." DeSimone gripped his shoulders with both hands.

"Get a hold of your client, counsel, or I'll remove him indefinitely from the hearing. Do you understand?" bellowed the judge.

"Yes, Your Honor, I understand." DeSimone could feel Nard's muscles begin to relax. "Come on, trust me. You gotta trust me."

"Court is adjourned until tomorrow at nine o'clock in the morning." The judge banged his gavel and the bailiff instructed the court to stand while the judge removed himself.

Barry Zone looked over at DeSimone, smiling like a sly fox. *You should have taken my plea offer when you had the chance. Yeah, you really should have taken that plea.* He knew DeSimone had to be thinking the same thing at that very moment. Of course Zone didn't say a word. Instead, he bent his head down and pretended to be sorting through his planner.

Who the fuck does this asshole think he's looking at? DeSimone fumed. He stood, grabbed his briefcase, and walked out of the courtroom. *What a day,* he thought as he answered his ringing cell phone. Just then a voice from behind him called out his name. He heard another person shouting in his direction. And he could also hear his fiancée demanding he respond to her on the other end of his oversized cell phone.

"Excuse me, Mr. DeSimone, one quick question?" said the voluptuous, blonde, and very attractive Gina Davenworth, who was hustling for her next paycheck.

"Hey, DeSimone, your client has no alibi. What do you think his outcome will be?" shouted another reporter from his left.

"Babe, I'll call you right back." DeSimone disconnected the call. "Do you guys mind? That was my girlfriend," he said as he stared at Gina Davenworth's breasts. If not for that one tiny button on her blouse, her perfect size Cs would pop right out of her shirt and say hello to him personally. As other reporters hovered and pushed one another, Davenworth's body pressed up against DeSimone's.

"Do you think your client will accept the DA's plea offer in light of today's testimony?" she asked from her soft-as-butter pink lips as she batted her baby blues at him.

"No comment," he huffed at her, rolling his eyes, before busting through the pack of hungry reporters, out the double glass doors of the courthouse, and onto the courthouse steps. *She wants me,* he thought to himself as he picked up his phone and dialed his fiancée back. He stood on the corner of Thirteenth Street. He looked up at the sky as he heard her answer.

"Hey, babe, I think I just had the worst day of my life. You're not going to believe it. If I don't come up with a master plan, I'm gonna lose. I'm really gonna lose—big. And I never lose, Jo. You know I never lose."

"I know, Bobby, I know," was all she could say. Joanne offered a sympathetic ear and listened carefully to his every word. She was of course genuinely interested, but Bobby made the final call on everything, including her.

"I've got to get home and go back through this case. There has to be a way to get this kid off… There's got to be."